Pearl Hart
& the
Violent Men

Also by Lee Martin

Shadow on the Mesa
Fast Ride to Boot Hill
The Last Wild Ride
The Grant Conspiracy: Wake of the Civil War
Fury at Cross Creek
In Mysterious Ways
Revenge at Rawhide
The Maverick Gun
Fury at Sweetwater Pass
The Lone Rider
Black River
Dead Man's Trail
Valley of the Lawless
Track the Men Down
The Danger Trail
Hang Town
Dead Man's Creek
Ride the Wild Wind
The Siege at Rhyker's Station
The Desperate Riders

The Darringer Brothers Series:

Trail of the Fast Gun
Trail of the Long Riders
Trail of the Hunter
Trail of the Circle Star
Trail of the Restless Gun
Trail of the Dangerous Gun

Pearl Hart & the Violent Men

LEE MARTIN

Vaca Mountain Press
Vacaville, California, U.S.A.

Vaca Mountain Press
Paperback ISBN 13: 978-1-952380-69-3
Kindle ISBN 13: 978-1-952380-70-9

Also available in:
Large Print Paperback ISBN 13: 978-1-952380-71-6

Cover and interior design by
Deirdre Wait, High Pines Creative
Cover images © Getty Images

Published by Vaca Mountain Press
Vacaville, California, U.S.A.

Visit Lee Martin Westerns on Facebook.

To all of my wonderful family,
and in memory of
my dear sister and best friend,
our beloved mother,
our rough-riding brothers,
and for Jim Liontas.

CHAPTER ONE

In 1910, Taft was president; calls for prohibition were beginning to sound; Arizona and New Mexico seeking statehood; women still fighting for the vote; censorship of movies pending; gas buggies competing with horses and wagons; aviation gaining attention; and baseball, golf, dog shows, boxing, tennis, theater, and horse racing were even more popular than in prior years. In parts of the West, though, changes came more slowly.

* * * *

In New Mexico Territory in the summer of 1910, a brand-new shiny black Model T Ford rattled along a lonely dirt road in the late afternoon. A wet canvas water bag dangled on a manila rope from the radiator cap. The puffing, noisy vehicle moved through open country with golden grasslands spread out in all directions. In the far north, crimson and yellow bluffs rose against the clear blue of the sky.

The driver, Elmer Kitchen—mid-twenties, pink-faced, with

light brown eyes—was looking like a dude in his straw hat with its red band, a red-and-white polka-dot bow tie, and his striped blue jacket with tan britches. He had high hopes as he pulled up to a wooden gate held by a board fence that stretched east and west for miles until no longer visible.

"Here I go," he said out loud with bravado. "I can do this."

Over the gate, an arched sign read: BEAR SPRINGS RANCH.

He got out to open the gate, drove through, and dutifully stepped out to close it behind him. All the while, his vehicle huffed and puffed and rattled. He climbed back behind the wheel and looked to his right, where he could see tall cottonwoods lining the banks of a creek and squirrels scattering as a red-tailed hawk sailed the sky.

He switched gears, and the Ford cast a cloud of smoke behind it.

"I'll be famous," he said, trying to up his courage.

Elmer drove on toward the distant ranch house. Painted white, it was long and single-level with a white picket fence around a garden of red, white, and yellow flowers. Behind the house, he could see a chicken coop with busy red hens behind a wire fence.

Further on, the reluctant blades of a windmill turned slowly in the breeze. Near it, he could see a vegetable garden with a scarecrow wearing a hat like his.

"That's a good sign," he said aloud of the hat, "I think."

Beyond the house, the dirt road continued on to a big red barn, sheds and corrals, with two bay horses nipping at each other over a fence. Further north, white-faced cattle could be seen on the grassy hills that were golden over red earth, rolling all the way to a distant tree line of dark pines.

Near the herd, two riders on sorrels reined up. They appeared to be teenagers, a girl and a younger boy. She wore split riding skirts, her long black hair flowing from under her wide brimmed hat. Now they rode off at a lope, heading over a hill and out of sight.

Elmer Kitchen pulled to a noisy halt near the picket fence. He turned off the gas engine, his vehicle shaking from the shock of it. The sudden silence drained his courage.

"God, help me," he prayed.

He saw the forty-eight-year-old rancher sitting on the covered porch in a large wooden chair. On the rancher's left, a table was set with a big pitcher of lemonade and glasses. On the other side of the table was another chair.

Elmer was afraid. He had never tackled anything like this before.

"Be careful, the sheriff said," Elmer mumbled aloud. "Be careful."

Now he could hear the chickens cackling behind the house and the creaking of the windmill. A gentle breeze caressed the sweat on his brow. He used a white handkerchief to wipe his face before stepping out of the Ford.

The rancher was a big man—at least six feet two inches tall with wide shoulders—with greying red-brown hair, clean-shaven, and ruggedly handsome. He wore a red plaid shirt, Levis, and worn, tan boots. Pushed back on his head was a stained tan Stetson with a wide brim. He looked like someone who enjoyed working on his ranch, but he also looked like the sheriff had said—a man you didn't rile.

A Winchester repeating rifle leaned near the front door.

Next to the rancher lay a huge white dog, a Great Pyrenees,

related to St. Bernards, but fluffier, taller, and bright-eyed.

Elmer waved to the rancher, who did not respond. With his briefcase in hand, Elmer headed through the gate and moved slowly up the stone path.

The white dog rose big and threatening with a gruff, booming bark.

"It's okay, Ben," the rancher said to the dog, his right hand on its neck.

"Wow," Elmer said, stopping short of the porch, "that's a Great Pyrenees, isn't it? Did you know they were named the Royal Dog of France?"

"I don't know about France, but here, they scare off predators. One bark and coyotes run for cover."

Elmer grinned. "I almost did. Could break an ear drum."

"They also like to play hide and seek."

"If I ever retire to the country, maybe I'll get one."

"Ben, here, he has nine new pups over at my neighbor's."

"I'm afraid the city's no place for one."

The rancher signaled Ben to lay back down, and Elmer, pausing now on the single step, continued with his mission.

"Mr. Donovan? I'm Elmer Kitchen, freelance writer from New York. I'm writing a documentary, a history, about lawmen and outlaws on the old southwest frontier. It will be serialized in the *Saturday Evening Post*. A big break for me."

The rancher studied him for a long moment.

Starting to lose his nerve, Elmer swallowed hard. "Over in town, the sheriff said you actually knew a lot of the bad men in those days, and he said you even knew Pearl Hart."

"Have a seat and some lemonade."

"Thank you, sir." Elmer made himself at home and sat in the

empty chair opposite the rancher, who gestured to the glasses and pitcher.

Glad to catch his breath, Elmer put his briefcase down and poured himself some lemonade. He took a pleasured sip before continuing.

"I heard that Pearl and her son and daughter disappeared a few years back. The kids were supposed to be in school back east. But I can't find any trace of a Nellie Hart or Freddy Hart."

The rancher sipped his own lemonade and didn't respond.

"Mr. Donovan, I…"

"Chance will do."

Elmer choked on his lemonade. "My gosh, you're Chance Donovan? The famous lawman who cleaned up the frontier? All those dime novels say you were worse than the outlaws you shot down or arrested! They called you the Iron Ranger in Texas, and the Iron Lawman in Arizona Territory. A giant who had no feelings whatsoever." Elmer caught himself. "I'm sorry, but I got excited."

Chance stared off into space as Elmer continued.

"Everyone's heard a hundred stories about Pearl Hart, but no one knows about you except from newspapers and those novels. Wow, if I get your true story, you can make me famous!"

Chance looked reluctant, so Elmer was more careful.

"If you help me, I promise to write your history just as you say, and before it's published, you can read it and make corrections. I'll stay with the truth, including whatever you remember about Pearl. Or where she is now."

Chance had had a lot of practice in reading men, so he nodded. "On one condition: that no one knows I have a ranch now or where it is, not even what territory, and you don't give the name or brand. I don't want anyone tracking me. Or her."

"Agreed! I promise no one will know where you are. And I sure don't want anyone to come here and steal from my success."

Chance nodded and sipped his own lemonade.

"Before we start," Elmer said, "I read you were an orphan adopted by a Texas Ranger, Robert Donovan. But do you know anything of your birth parents? What was your birth name?"

"Wesley Grant. My father died in the War Between the States. My mother remarried but she died when I was twelve."

Elmer started to ask more, but Chance held up his hand to stop him.

"Okay. The newspaper said that your adoptive father was shot down in Texas, back in 1893. Is that why you left and took a badge in Arizona Territory?"

Chance nodded but was getting annoyed. "I regret ever talking to that reporter."

"I promise you won't feel that way when you read my story."

Chance wore an uncertain expression on his face.

Elmer continued, trying to soften the exchange. "Can we start with the truth about Pearl Hart? There are so many interviews and conflicting reports. Maybe you'll feel more inclined to let me include more about your life as we go along. That's what will make me famous. She's old news. You're not."

Chance appeared to be having regrets about the interview.

Elmer managed to sip some lemonade, then set it aside and opened his briefcase, taking out pencils and a fat tablet. He tried to be careful with his questions.

"Pearl seems to have disappeared in the last few years, and the sheriff said you might tell me how to find her."

Chance reached down to put his right hand on his dog's neck.

The day was getting hotter, but the wind had risen and reached them in the shade.

Elmer wiped his brow. "Did you know her back when she robbed the stage and went to Yuma prison?"

Chance nodded but remained silent.

Sensing the rancher's resistance, Elmer slowed down. He knew if he got Chance to open up about Pearl Hart, it would be easier to feed in questions about the lawman's life without aggravating him, but as the sheriff had warned, Elmer had to be careful.

Elmer shuffled papers. "I have never met Pearl Hart, but I already have a lot of information from the courts. And Yuma. And I read her interview in Cosmopolitan and some others she did a few years ago. Anything you can tell me will help because there were a lot of news stories saying really bad things about her."

Chance frowned and waited for the often-heard question.

"So, was she really a prostitute?"

"You ask me that again and this visit is over and done."

Elmer swallowed his surprise and shrunk from the hot anger in Chance's angry gaze. "Sorry, I guess that's a no, and I'm glad to have an answer. I just wanted to dispel the rumors, so, thanks."

Chance backed off and didn't respond.

"Okay, so can I start taking notes?" Elmer asked.

"All right."

"Can you tell me where you first met her?"

"Phoenix."

Elmer spread out his papers and sorted the handwritten pages. "I was just in Phoenix. Did you know they have over 300 gas buggies now? They even raised the speed limit to 12 mph. Not really safe on the street. Over 11,000 people. And they even shut down the red-light district. They just want to show off the opera house. And culture."

"Interesting."

"So, she was in Phoenix. When was that?"

"Summer. 1898."

"Twelve years ago. That the year of the Spanish–American War?"

"Yes."

"Her husband was Fred Hart, a drummer. Didn't he run off and join the Rough Riders? Do you know why a dandy like him would do that?"

"He was afraid he'd be arrested."

"Wow. Are you going tell me why?"

"Later."

Elmer fussed. "That war only lasted to August of that same year. Did he come back?"

Chance nodded but didn't elaborate.

"Did he get arrested?"

"Not then."

Getting frustrated, Elmer realized Chance would only lay out the story in his own good time. He had to accept that.

Elmer shuffled papers. "Okay, so let's start in summer, 1898, before he joined up, right? He was still around when you met her?"

"Yes, he was."

"That's when she was working as a cook at the Liberty Hotel and Saloon, and scrubbing floors, just for room and board. One interview, she said that Fred Hart was a gambler who was always broke and often abusive. Once, he even knocked her unconscious. She said he sold every bit of jewelry she had except her mother's gold locket. But why would she let him?"

Chance shrugged but didn't answer.

"Unless she loved him, like she said. And I read how her church didn't allow for divorce."

Chance sipped his lemonade in silence.

Elmer scribbled. "Okay, and he forced her to sing because the hotel and saloons paid her well and men threw money at her. I know at times she was in a choir. Did you ever hear her sing?"

Chance nodded, but offered no comment.

"I hear she wasn't very tall."

"Neither is a bobcat."

"You're saying she was feisty?"

Chance grinned, briefly, and nodded.

"Yuma records say her eyes were grey, but others said they were blue."

"Sky-blue. Got darker when she was mad."

"She was a brunette," Elmer added.

Chance nodded agreement. He looked past Elmer at the teenagers still riding around the hills. He adjusted his hat and shifted in his chair for more comfort.

Elmer, barely able to control his excitement, started writing in a fresh, new tablet.

"Okay, lets start with when you first met her."

With great reflection, Chance went back in time with his story as Elmer filled in the gaps in his manuscript.

CHAPTER TWO

In summer of 1898, McKinley was president, the United States was already at war with Spain over Cuba, and there was active recruiting for the Rough Riders.

Women had been riding mens' saddles in split skirts for several years, but the sidesaddle was still considered more lady-like and believed less likely to harm their ability to have children, later found to be a myth. Women also continued to fight for the vote. Suffragettes, including Pearl Hart, were mostly ignored.

*   *   *   *

In that summer of 1898, Phoenix was a bustling metropolis with several railroads, telephones that sometimes worked, and electric street cars. The stagecoach still traveled to and from locations far from the set route of the rails. Autos wouldn't arrive for another two years, but Phoenix was fast on it's way to being the most exciting town in the territory. The red-light district was now illegal. With an opera house, newspapers, churches, a new library movement, and well-dressed ladies, it was the place to be. In another year, it was expected the capitol would move there from Prescott.

*   *   *   *

A long distance and hours from town, Deputy U.S. Marshal Chance Donovan had spent the night in the desert with wind and passing rain. He sat by his campfire under a sagging tarp and enjoyed a strong cup of coffee. The rising sun was in and out of lingering clouds, casting its light across the silver sage. Dark clouds, with flashes of lightning, hovered over the mountains in the north.

His camp was among the near-leafless palo verde, which had supported the tarp over his bedding, its branches providing a break from the pungent chips in his fire. During the night, the glassy eyes of some critter had caught the firelight for a long while before it left in the rain. He had heard an owl in the sycamores further up the trail and the flutter of night birds. Cold and wet, he felt a shiver run down his right leg and stood up.

His buckskin gelding, black mane and tail sagging, stood with its head down, black-tipped ears laid back in disapproval. The tarp over him had slid sideways.

"Sorry, Sam," he said.

Thirty-six with deep, blue eyes and dark, auburn hair under a black Stetson, Chance had big shoulders and stood six-feet two-inches tall. His size alone was intimidating. Dressed all in black with a red bandanna, he wore a brass badge in the shape of a star. It read 'U. S. Deputy Marshal, Arizona Territory'. It was pinned on his vest but only seen when his long coat spread to the side. On his right hip was a holstered Army Colt.

A lonely man who had never married, Chance was on his own with no family or close friends. Haunted by nightmares since he was a boy, he often saw the same misery in the flickering red and yellow flames of his campfire.

When he was twelve, he had seen his mother die in a fall down the stairs, thanks to his drunken stepfather. He had ridden off into the night, bareback on an old bay gelding, while his stepfather fired crazily from the barn. Shot in the back of his left shoulder, he had hunched down with his fist full of mane and had disappeared into the desert where he expected to die without food or water.

Alone and frightened, near death, he prayed.

The next morning, having been thrown, he had lain on his side in the sand, certain he would die in the hot sun, until a strong voice had caused him to look up at a giant of a lawman.

"Well, son, I guess you could use a hand."

His adoptive father, the Texas Ranger who had found him in the desert "by chance" and so named him, was the finest man Chance had ever known. Until the ranger had been murdered five years ago, with the crime unsolved, leaving a lingering misery.

The only way to live with it all was to do his job, which was all-consuming.

He walked over to give his horse some grain. "Time to go, Sam."

The buckskin nudged him, then ate from the sack.

He broke camp under a cloudy sky with flashes of sunlight. He forced himself to ride back into civilization. It was late morning when he reached Phoenix. Not many folks were out because of the damp and the threat of rain lingering. A few saddle horses stood at railings, and farmer's wagons, already unloaded, stood near the store fronts.

The street cars were back in a shelter, leaving the rails to sit in the mud.

As he rode Sam along the muddy street toward the distant Liberty Hotel, a green and white two-story building, he yearned for some decent hot coffee. He usually stayed at the Stockman's, but it was on the other side of town and he was thirsty and hungry.

Two eight-year-old boys playing on the boardwalk jumped up and pointed stick pistols at him. They were rough-and-tumble, mischievous, flush-faced, wearing overalls and worn boots. No hats. Just fluffy brown hair and big brown eyes.

They shouted, "Bang! Bang!"

Chance grinned, tipped his hat, and kept riding as the boys disappeared down an alley behind them.

It was a lonely man's dream to have sons like that. He had often wondered if he would ever find the right woman, let alone that she would even want him.

He reined up to look around, wondering where the boys had gone. His horse's hooves were deep in the muck. He waved back to a rancher across the street.

Finally, he rode on past the next alley, unaware of a man watching from the shadows. Joe Boot—a thirty-year-old handsome dude in dark suit and hat, flashy red vest, and silver inlaid gunbelt—wore a thin, dark brown mustache. He moved back a step as the lawman rode past. He waited until he was sure Chance wouldn't look back and couldn't hear him.

13

Unaware of the two youngsters coming up behind him in the alley, Joe leaned slightly into the light. He pointed his finger like a pistol at Chance's back and muttered in a low voice, *"Bang."*

The boys behind him loved it, pointed their pistols at Joe's back and shouted, "Bang! Bang!"

So startled he almost wet himself, Joe spun, angry, swung at the boys and missed.

The boys giggled, ran back down the alley and out of sight as they circled back to another alley but didn't enter. Instead, they turned and ran across a muddy field toward the livery, looking for more mischief, if they could find it.

Joe, badly shaken, wiped his brow and stayed in the alley for a time.

Not having seen Joe or the man's encounter with the boys, Chance Donovan soon turned his big buckskin over toward the hitching rail at the Liberty Hotel and Saloon. Many horses were already at the rail. As the sun began to shine full time, a half dozen men and women further down the street were entering a café. Merchants were opening their doors and hanging out samples, some boots and some hats.

Chance reined to a halt at the sound of commotion from inside the Liberty.

He heard angry shouts from men in the dining room, which he knew was to the left of the main entrance of the hotel. He heard furniture being tossed about and a lot of men cussing.

Out of the hotel's big, double oak doors came Pearl Hart, a pretty, twenty-eight-year-old young woman, her long, dark brown hair tied back with a ribbon. Wearing a full-length white bib apron over a blue print dress with high collar and rolled up sleeves, she stumbled to the edge of the boardwalk.

She seemed not to notice Chance, still mounted to her left.

At sight of the muddy street which still had standing water in spots, she hesitated. It was that or be caught on the boardwalk in either direction.

Behind her, an intoxicated Fred Hart—thirty-four years old with dark brown hair and eyes, wearing a thin mustache, and dressed like a gambler in fancy clothes—grabbed her from behind. He jerked her around, then slapped her hard. He tried to get at the gold locket she clasped in her left hand, the chain still around her throat.

"Let me go!" she squealed, fighting back.

A half dozen men, ranchers and town merchants, came out behind him, intent on helping Pearl. Hart turned, drew his pistol and shook it at them, making them back off.

"Leave her alone, Hart!" one shouted.

"Yeah, Fred, let her go," another warned.

"She's my wife!"

"We ain't lettin' you hit her no more," a big man said.

Pearl tried to get free but Hart gripped her left wrist.

He kept the men back by continuing to wave his pistol.

"You're drunk, Hart," one man said. "Let her go."

He tried again for the gold locket. She kicked him in the left shin. He cussed.

Pearl broke free, stepped back off the boardwalk and into the muddy street. Still upright, she kept backing away, soft shoes and skirts sucking up mud and water. She tried to turn around to cross over, lost her balance before she could, and grabbed air as she fell forward. She dropped to her knees in the deep, wet mud and splashing water, still facing her husband. She was a good six feet from his reach.

Hart stepped to the edge of the boardwalk, not so drunk he would wade into the mud. "Get back inside!" he said.

Too hurt to stand and dragged down by her skirts, Pearl turned on her hands and knees. She crawled through the mud toward the center of the street.

Hart continued to yell at her. "Stop right there!"

One of the men behind Hart slipped up close, put his boot on the gambler's rear and shoved.

Hart yelped, fell crazily forward, free of the boardwalk, and landed on his belly, his gun still in his right hand but deep in the mud. He got up and staggered after his wife. He was barely able to stay upright as he kicked at her from behind. She turned around and tried to shove his boot away.

Now she grabbed at it and twisted his leg. He yelped and kicked.

She let go, and he fell back on his rear in the mud, then sat up.

Now they were facing each other on hands and knees.

Hart managed to stand again but was unaware of Chance moving over on his buckskin. Hart kicked at her face and missed as she kept slithering backwards on her hands and knees.

Chance leaned down and popped Hart on his head with his left fist.

Hart fell back to his knees, stunned, furious.

Pearl didn't look up at Chance. She just had to get away and turned, crawling again towards the center of the street, but not making much progress.

Hart, bleary-eyed from drink, staggered to his feet again. He looked up to see the badge. It was a blur at first, then a shining star in the sun.

Intoxicated, with a guilty conscience and sudden fear, Hart

panicked and aimed his muddied pistol up at Chance. He pulled the trigger. The gun exploded in his right hand and threw mud in his face. He staggered back, his hand in shock, but remained on his feet.

In a wild frenzy, Hart dropped but then reclaimed the damaged weapon in his left hand. He turned and fought his way onto the boardwalk as the crowd laughed and backed away. He stumbled on down the street, away from them and Chance. Further on, he slipped and slid, then disappeared down the closest alley.

One of the men, a burly rancher, followed him to the alley entrance to track him, then returned and addressed Chance, who had dismounted and secured his buckskin at the rail.

"He's headed for the livery," the rancher said. "We'll get the police after him. Or maybe Sheriff Truman, if he's in town. Unless you want him?"

Chance shook his head. Standing in slush himself, he was more interested in Pearl, muddied and on her hands and knees, still trying to get across the street. She looked so darn cute crawling in the muck, he took his time.

Two of the men on the boardwalk started to remove their coats in order to step into the deep mud for a rescue. Chance waved them back. This was going to be a bit of fun, something he had not had for many years.

She tried to get up but slipped and fell again face down on her elbows.

Chance moved over to her as she rose up on her hands again. He bent down and picked her up by wrapping his left arm around her waist. She squealed.

He threw her over his left shoulder, his arm holding her legs.

Dangling down his back, she started beating him with her fists. He had the urge to pat her on the rear but thought better of it.

She didn't know who he was or that he had chased off her husband. She was too high up with her waist on his shoulder to have seen his face or the badge. She felt like she was being hauled off by a giant.

"Put me down, you big poop!"

Chance grinned as the men made way for him and gave grinning approval.

He walked through the big open doors and into the empty but well-furnished lobby of the hotel. It was plush with deep beige carpet, red stuffed chairs, and walnut coffee tables. Red velvet drapes were everywhere.

Pearl was still dangling over his left shoulder, pounding on his back.

He saw the lounge—actually a fancied-up saloon—to his right, the busy dining room to his left, and the red carpeted stairs straight ahead. He stopped at the desk where a short, grey-haired man with round spectacles was chuckling.

"She needs a bath," Chance said, trying not to grin.

"Top of the stairs, Room 1. The tub's being filled for a male guest."

"He can wait."

"You big ox! Put me down!" Pearl cried, beating on his back.

Chance carried her up the stairs and onto the landing.

She kept pounding on him with her fists. He hauled her down along the landing and into the open door of the wash room.

A young Mexican maid in white dress and apron was standing at a table with towels in her arms. She set them down and giggled at the intrusion.

A large, deep, metal tub, steaming with hot water, was waiting against a side wall, half hidden by a blue curtain. The maid smiled at Chance, who had entered with the frantic Pearl.

"Get her shoes," Chance said.

The maid pulled off Pearl's soaked shoes and stockings, dodging the kicks, but fretted about the muddy skirts of Pearl's dress and apron.

"Get her some clean clothes," Chance said.

Pearl squirmed. "Let me go! I don't need your help, you big tub of lard!"

Chance plunked her down in the deep metal tub, clothes and all. Water splashed up and around her, up to her shoulders.

She gasped, tried to get up, and failed. Water spiraled out onto the hardwood floor.

Chance paused, faked a grimace, looked down at her. "I catch you in the mud again, I'll arrest you."

She tried to rise, sank, and splashed. She glared up at Chance, seeing his badge for the first time. She quickly realized why her husband had run away.

Then she saw Chance's handsome face, the clean-shaven, strong jaw, his friendly eyes and sudden grin. Breathless, she sat stunned as he tipped his hat and left, closing the door behind him.

Pearl was breathless, in shock, but enamored. "Wow!"

The maid laughed, and nodded agreement.

In the hallway, Chance saw a rough-looking bearded man in a dirty work outfit, possibly a miner, with a change of clothes over his arm, coming toward him. He took one look at Chance's badge, and he spun and went back down the hall.

Chance grinned, then sobered, as he returned to the stairs and went down into the still-empty lobby. He walked to the desk as the clerk waved him over with a chuckle.

"You know who that was, marshal? Pearl Hart."

Chance nodded and adjusted his hat.

"She's one of them suffragettes. You know, they want the vote. But women just ain't fit for politics. They got their place, barefoot and pregnant, and they oughta stay in it. But they just never stop yakking and complaining."

Chance was amused. "Did you tell her that?"

The clerk had to laugh. "Are you kidding? I'm not that brave."

Chance was more serious as he walked out of the entrance to check on his horse. He could not remember a time when a woman had made him smile. Pearl had shaken him from head to toe. He could still feel her on his shoulder, pounding on his back and calling him names. He had stayed alone in his life, by choice, but she had stirred new feelings. She was pretty and full of life, a joy for any man—but, sadly, she was already married.

Meanwhile, up in the wash room, Pearl had stripped and was enjoying a hot bath with the maid's help. A change of clothes now waited on a chair.

"Who was that big brute?" Pearl finally asked from behind the curtain.

"He is Marshal Donovan."

"The one who shot those bank robbers in Tucson?"

"I don't know. But I also think he is 'wow'."

Pearl laughed.

But then she felt painfully sad. '*It doesn't matter. I'll never be free.*'

CHAPTER THREE

After he was done chatting with the desk clerk, Chance walked through the lobby where he heard Pearl's rescuers laughing in the dining room to his right.

Needing a moment to himself, he continued outside and stood on the boardwalk in the sunlight. Dark clouds still hovered low on the mountains in the north. It was late morning and he was in need of some strong coffee and a hot meal.

Many citizens were now out and about, enjoying the clear weather. Ladies held their parasols tight in the wind.

A wagon down the street was being unloaded by an Apache and his wife, who wore colorful clothes. They were carrying their goods inside the general store as two little boys, wearing white headbands like their father, trailed behind them.

Many men and women did marry and have families, he reminded himself.

Chance felt light-hearted for the first time ever. Pearl had made him laugh and remember how, as a small boy, he and others his size had chased muddy pigs at the county fair to win a prize. Seeing Pearl sliding around in the mud and yet keeping her grit, not crying, just being feisty—that was to be admired.

Chance had accepted he would never be able to settle down. He had shut himself off from the world, had buried his emotions deep. Yet, a muddy woman had pierced his shell. A married woman, at that, which put her out of reach—and that was painful to acknowledge. The image of her in the bathtub in her clothes, snippy with anger, still tickled him... but it could never be, and that hurt.

He felt a chill run through him, despite the warm sun.

Standing in the sunlight with his hat brim shading his face, he told himself he had to get out of this town and not come back anytime soon. Seeing her, knowing she was unavailable, was too heavy on his heart.

Except, he was mighty hungry and thirsty for coffee. He scraped more mud from his boots on the warped edge of the boardwalk.

He turned to watch as County Sheriff Bill Truman—a likeable and husky greying man in his fifties—came down the boardwalk. He didn't wear any kind of uniform, just a long grey coat, tan clothes, and a badge on his vest. He stopped near where Chance stood by his big buckskin. Chance loosened the cinch, hooked the stirrup on the horn, then moved back onto the boardwalk.

Truman reached out and shook Chance's hand. "I just heard a funny story about Fred Hart chasing his wife around in the mud, down on their knees. And how he tried to shoot up at you when his pistol exploded in his hand. Liveryman just told me he lit out so fast, he almost outran his horse. Want to go after him?"

Chance grinned and shook his head as Truman continued.

"And then I heard how you picked up Mrs. Hart and hauled her into the hotel, mud and all, and dropped her into a tub of hot water."

"She needed a bath."

Truman chuckled. "I wish I had seen it."

They stood awhile longer on the boardwalk in the bright sun.

Chance stretched and looked toward the hotel. "Sure could use some hot coffee."

"Want some real Texas Chili?"

"In the dining room? Kind of fancy."

"Not that fancy. And Pearl's a good cook."

"They been around here long?"

Truman pushed his hat back. "Fred Hart had split a couple times when they were elsewhere, and she came here on her own. She got a job working for the hotel, mostly as a cook, which included room and board. He showed up only a few weeks ago. Gambled away every penny she'd saved. He got her a job singing in the hotel saloon, or lounge, as they call it. She gets a heap of money thrown at her. He gambles it as fast as she can earn it. But the more she fights back at Hart, the worse it gets. You sure scared him off, though, so maybe he won't be back."

Chance thought about it, waited as Truman continued.

"They have little kids, a boy and a girl, but she sent them to her mother in Canada."

"I can see why."

"And just so you know, there's a fellah been hanging around of late. Joe Boot. I seen him do some exhibition shooting in Denver once. Fastest draw I ever did see. Never missed. But he's been pretty quiet around here."

23

"That so?" Chance shrugged.

"Mostly, he just plays cards, or sits in the dark and watches Pearl when she's singing nights in the hotel lounge. But he did ask the barkeep if you were coming back to town."

"Maybe he has a guilty conscience."

"Like Fred Hart?" Truman laughed, then sobered.

In the Liberty Hotel's busy dining room, Chance and Truman sat at a table near the front window with its parted red drapes. The outer glass was smeared from the storm.

Still, they could see outside where couples strolled by in the bright sun; kids playing on the boardwalk but venturing out into the mud when no one was watching; and cowboys riding into town.

Inside, there were a dozen tables, all crowded with merchants and ranchers, along with one prim lady in a feathered bonnet and her well-dressed husband.

Their waiter was a smiling elderly man who brought them coffee and took their orders for chili. On their table with the plates and tableware, there was a tall pitcher of cream, from which Truman helped himself for his coffee.

They could glimpse Pearl in the back where she was working in the busy kitchen.

Truman was surprised. "She sure cleaned up fast."

Freshly bathed, her dark hair tied back with a red ribbon, wearing a clean blue print dress and white bib apron, she seemed cheerful and talkative with the kitchen staff. She also looked as pretty as ever.

In the kitchen, she kept smiling. Her cheer came from learning that Fred Hart had left town in a hurry. She also could not forget the big handsome lawman who had rescued her from the mud. That experience had sparked a bit of joy in her. However, he had also embarrassed her and was right pushy about it, so she knew she would have to get even, sooner or later.

She ventured out with a coffee pot to refill diners' cups, dodging cowboys' sneaky hands. Her gold locket dangled from the white collar of her dress.

Chance, already on his way to being smitten, watched her move about. She had darkening bruises on her face. Her sore left arm was hard to lift, so she kept the coffee pot in her right hand. Men flirted with her, making her laugh.

She paused at sight of Chance and Truman. There was the target of her planned revenge. She braced herself, then walked over to them to refill their coffee cups.

Chance looked up at her with a grin, nodded his thanks. She gave him a nasty smirk and returned to the kitchen to handle orders for chili.

"Oh, oh," Truman said. "You'd better be careful what she serves you."

Pearl, our of sight in the kitchen, took one bowl of the chili destined for their table and smiled. She stirred red hot pepper sauce into it. She put both bowls on a tray but smeared chili on the side of Chance's bowl to mark it.

Trying not to give herself away, she fought back a smile and returned to serve Chance and Truman, making sure Chance got the doctored bowl.

Chance stared into the chili, which was definitely redder than expected. He sniffed and looked up at her testy smile. She served Truman his bowl, and waited.

Chance tasted the chili, nodded with approval, and began eating.

"Wow," he said, "this is great."

He downed several mouthfuls of it as she watched, amazed and disappointed.

Pearl shook her head as she turned away.

Chance watched her disappear into the kitchen. His mouth and insides on fire, he grabbed the pitcher of cream and downed it as fast as he could.

"She likes you," Truman said, grinning.

"I hope she doesn't get to love me," Chance gasped, sipping the last of the cream.

Truman signaled the waiter, who came to replace the pitcher.

Chance then had a few more swallows of cream as Truman grinned.

At that point, Lester Locke, a well-dressed man in his sixties with scruffy grey hair and beard, showed up and went over to Truman and Chance, who welcomed him to sit at their table. The waiter took his order and left.

"How are things at the diggings?" Truman asked.

"Rich, but there's a lot more water showing up in the tunnels," Lester said. "They pump, but it's a worry. The copper is getting a lot of attention because there's so much of it wrapped around the silver. The stamp mill is down the way about five miles near the smelter, which has some problems. But no one is giving up."

The noise of the diners rose with some laughter at joke-telling among a group of ranch hands at a far table. The smell of great food in the kitchen drifted out often among the customers.

After a time, the waiter brought Lester his coffee and chili.

Lester was quickly amazed. "This is the best chili ever."

"The cook's a dandy," Truman said. "Pearl Hart."

"A woman? Is she married?"

"Separated," Truman replied. "Chance scared 'im off."

Chance ignored the remark and sipped his coffee as the waiter picked up their chili bowls, noting Chance had not emptied his. The man soon returned with hot apple pie. Chance lifted the crust to look for signs of salt but didn't see any.

Truman chuckled at Chance's caution.

They enjoyed the fresh apple pie, which was still warm.

When Pearl returned with coffee refills, she saw that the second pitcher of cream was almost empty. She was expecting a complaint, but Chance just smiled, looking unshaken by the chili.

"That was great apple pie," Truman said.

She smiled her thanks and ignored Chance's grin.

"Mrs. Hart," Lester said, "I'm Lester Locke. I got a food service and some cabins up at East Ridge mining camp up in the mountains, north of here. Lots of silver up there. I'm serving some sixty miners at a time. I got some new competition down the road, and my cook wants to quit and get back in town. So, I need a new one."

Pearl was immediately interested because she was still afraid her abusive husband might return. The hotel kitchen staff could take over for her at anytime.

Lester continued. "I'd pay you double. Even give you a place to live. Ain't much more'n a shack, but the door locks."

Pearl set the pot on the table. "When can I start?"

"Soon's you get there. I'm heading back today. I suggest you ride up with the mail wagon tomorrow morning. You'll see my place right off."

"I'll be there," she said.

Truman gestured. "You know, she can sing real pretty, too."

Lester brightened. "Well, maybe we can work something out, get you even more pay."

She looked pleased as she poured more coffee for Chance, still watching for steam to come out of his ears, but he just smiled up at her. As much as she wanted to get even, she couldn't forget his rescuing her from the mud, nor his strength and humor. She regretted never having such a man in her life.

She left the coffee pot on their table and turned away. She yanked off her apron and crumbled it. She headed for the lobby, intending to resign at the desk and go upstairs to pack.

A burly miner turned in his chair, reached out, and grabbed at her rear.

She spun and threw the apron in his face. As he clawed at it, she grabbed his nose and twisted it. The miner yelped.

Pearl smiled sweetly as she let go. "Sorry, mister, but that was the last straw."

The miner tossed off the apron, leaned back, rubbed his sore nose, and grinned.

"No offense, ma'am."

Laughter followed her as she walked out of the dining room.

Chance left coins on the table, said goodbye to Truman and Lester. They grinned after him as he walked away.

"Chance getting himself into trouble?" Lester asked.

"Yeah, he just doesn't know it yet," Truman replied with a chuckle.

Chance followed Pearl into the empty lobby, hat in hand.

She was at the desk, telling the old man behind it that she was quitting.

"My helpers can do the cooking from now on," she said. "Can I pick up my pay before I leave tomorrow?"

"I'll make sure of it," the clerk said, adjusting his spectacles.

Then she turned to stare up at Chance with a forced scowl.

"You big overgrown stump. I'm still mad at you."

"That so?"

"Did you like your chili?" she asked with a sudden giggle.

He nodded seriously. "Sure did."

"I bet your insides are on fire. Are you proPearly put in your place?" she asked.

She smiled up at him and looked so darn cute, Chance suddenly found himself tongue-tied.

Pearl persisted. "Yes?"

Chance still could not find his voice. He pulled his hat on, adjusted and tipped it, then hurriedly turned away. He exited the double doors into the sunlight.

Pearl stood quiet for a long moment, glaring after him, and then smiled.

Sheriff Truman, hat in hand, came into the lobby and walked with her to the front windows to look out. They were not in earshot of anyone. They saw Chance at his buckskin, tightening the cinch and dropping the stirrup.

"You got him buffaloed?" he asked with a grin.

"He's a real stone-face. I poured half a bottle of red pepper sauce into his chili. He didn't even flinch! What kind of man is that?"

"A man with a hot mouth." Truman chuckled, then sobered. "He's a good man, Pearl. But he carries a lot of misery."

Pearl hesitated, fell silent as he continued.

"I heard he was once a skinny little runaway orphan adopted

by a Texas Ranger, and then he grew up to be one of 'em. And bigger'n most." He paused to reshape his hat, still in hand. "But the ranger who adopted him was shot down a few years ago. So, he has no family."

Pearl winced at the story. "Why did you have to tell me all that?"

"I'm sorry, I thought you liked him."

She shook her head. "Yes, I like him, and now I feel so bad for him, but what can I do about it?"

"He's never been married."

She flinched. "But *I* am. Fred always comes back. Like a bad penny."

"I know a lawyer who can help with a divorce."

"My family's church doesn't allow it. Anyway, I have no savings. Fred took it all," she said sadly. "And now I have another letter from my brother. He says my mother is still sick up in Canada. And I don't even have the fare to go see her."

Truman looked sad for her.

She sniffed back a tear and felt she could unload on his kind interest. "It's all my fault. I met Fred in Canada when I was sixteen, and I heard all his stories about the Wild West shows and how the frontier was full of adventure. So, rather than marry the storekeeper my parents had picked out for me, I eloped with Fred. At first, it was exciting, but it wasn't long before all he did was gamble, and lie, and beat on me when he was mad at the world."

Truman put a hand on her shoulder. "I'm sorry."

She tried to perk up and forced a grin. "But now I'll have a better job with Mr. Locke, so I can save up, if Fred doesn't come back and take it away from me. Assuming Mr. Locke keeps his word."

"Lester's a good man. You can trust him."

She dabbed at her tears. "You're so nice to me, sheriff."

"I'll look in on you at East Ridge."

"I would like that," she said, managing a smile.

"I will say one more thing. Chance Donovan has been bottled up all his life. Nothing has ever gotten to him that I've ever seen or heard of. But you shook the heck out of him."

"Am I that bad?"

She seemed ready again to blame herself for everything, because Fred had made sure she was always apologizing to him. The gold band on her finger had her trapped.

She waited for Truman's answer.

"To the contrary." He chuckled. "I think picking you out of the mud and hauling you to the wash room, that's probably the most fun he's had in years. Did he really set you down in a tub, clothes and all?"

"Yes, and I was mad, but not anymore."

"Don't give up," he said. "Only the good Lord knows what's ahead."

"Yes, I know, but it's nice to be reminded."

"Good luck."

She smiled as Truman donned his hat, then tipped it, and turned for the front entrance. Watching the sheriff leave, she sobered in her loneliness and misery.

She still had her son and daughter with family in Canada, because she had never wanted them to have to face anymore of Fred's explosive anger. Her yearning for adventure had got her into this fix in the first place, but all she wanted now was to find peace and safety, and a chance to earn enough to help her mother.

She was even more sad for her own self. Into her life had come a big man with a big grin who had stirred some kind of deep yearning in her soul.

Yet, she knew Fred Hart would show up again looking for gambling money, sooner or later. If only she could hide forever at the mining camp.

'*Dear God,*' she thought, '*please help me.*'

A tear trickled down her cheek as she turned to go back to the stairs.

Every step she took as she climbed up slowly took her breath away. On the landing, she stopped to rest and wiped more tears from her face.

CHAPTER FOUR

L ater that night in his office in Phoenix, Sheriff Truman
received a telegram, which he took to the livery where he
knew Chance was grooming his buckskin. The building was on
a back street with wide open front doors, full stalls, and outside
corrals with additional horses.

It was cold out, for the desert seldom held any heat from the
day.

Lamps burned on the walls inside the big barn. Some
cowhands and drifters were asleep in the lofts. Snoring could be
heard high above them. Some horses were asleep in their stalls.
Others pawed the straw from time to time.

Truman came over to Chance, who was combing the golden
buckskin, fussing with its black mane. Sam nosed Chance as if
wanting even more attention.

"You don't look like a man with good news," Chance said.

Truman was grim. "The Boxers broke out of prison in
Mexico."

They both considered the news for awhile before Chance spoke.

"They know which way they headed?"

"Telegram doesn't say. But Trey Boxer is the leader and the worst of the lot, and they still want him bad in Texas, so maybe they won't head north." Truman leaned on a post. "Didn't you have a run-in with a Boxer when you were with the Rangers?"

"Yeah, about five years ago, at a bank robbery in San Antonio. One of them I shot was Randy Boxer. We didn't know who he was until the sheriff told us, that he was Trey Boxer's brother. They had murdered people inside the bank, including a woman, so we didn't feel too bad about taking them down. All five of them."

"Do you think Trey knows who got his brother?"

"It was in the newspaper the next day."

Chance continued combing the buckskin, which often nosed him and even bit at him once. "Sam, behave yourself."

"That's one fine animal," Truman said, then was back to the news. "You ever run into Trey Boxer?"

For a moment, Chance remembered back to a time when he had been ready to hunt Trey down with a vengeance, but the tough Texas Ranger who had adopted him as a son had set him straight. "Do your duty," Robert Donovan had said, "and make things right when you can, but remember, you can't hate a blind man because he's blind. Men are what they are. We are not the judge or the jury. We wear a badge, not a robe."

Chance had kept his promise to follow the law, but it had not been easy.

He was aware Truman was waiting to hear if he knew Trey Boxer.

Chance hedged. "I'd only recognize him from his poster."

Truman had to drum up some courage to ask further.

"I hate to bring it up, but I know your father was shot down not long after that bank robbery. And his murder was never solved. Did that newspaper list your full name as the one who got Randy?"

"No, just Ranger Donovan. That's what it said on my report."

"Could the Boxers have thought your pa was the Donovan who killed Trey's brother?"

Chance winced. "I've asked myself that question many times."

"How would they have even known where he was?"

"Could be they were in El Paso where he had spent the night."

"And someone heard his name and he was followed?"

"Or it was a random attack on a lone traveler. Whoever shot him took his identification card. And his gold watch."

Truman sighed. "I guess it could have been anyone on the prod."

"My father had a lot of enemies."

"But if it was the Boxers, they would know from his Ranger's card and might have figured they got lucky."

Chance nodded as he offered Sam grain in a canvas nose bag. "Except, right after, the El Paso newspaper said he had been returning from testifying as a witness at a trial in Santa Fe. Where he had been at the same time as the bank robbery."

"So, if they read the newspaper…"

"Could be they didn't stick around to see it."

"Men like that are braggarts. If they read the San Antonio paper, they sure had their hands on the El Paso news. Which means, you had better watch yourself."

"I doubt they even know I left the Rangers. And they're on the run."

Truman could see the questions had caused Chance a great deal of stress, so he brought up a more cheery subject.

"I know you're staying at the Stockman's," Truman said, "but maybe we can go back to the Liberty by nine o'clock. Pearl will be singing one last time. Just a few songs, but her voice is right beautiful. I think she'd like us there."

"Yeah, maybe."

Chance couldn't admit he was almost afraid to hear her sing. He was already smitten with her, and she was still another man's wife.

But he gave in and walked from the livery with Truman. Lamps burned along the street. It was cold and still damp. The aging boardwalk seemed louder under their boots.

Chance had lived a hard, lonely life, but Pearl had put a song in his heart the minute he had set her down in that bathtub, clothes and all. The exasperated look on her face would stay with him forever. To watch her sing might be downright painful.

Inside the lobby of the Liberty Hotel, a sign read: *Lounge. Tables for Ladies.*

Chance and Truman found it was standing room only. They stayed just inside the entrance, out of the pale glow of the crystal chandelier. Ranchers, farmers, merchants and their ladies, all had crowded inside. Cowboys lined the far wall. Tables were small, rounded, and set with lighted candles.

The piano was on a platform some twenty feet away from where the lawmen stood in the shadows. A pair of candles on the black instrument added to the show.

There was applause as Pearl appeared on the platform, wearing a shiny blue dress with lace on the high collar and sleeves, her hair tied back with a shiny blue ribbon. She looked especially beautiful. It grew quiet as she put her hand on the piano for balance.

The piano player was a greying, clean-shaven man in his sixties. He sat down and rested his fingers on the keys. Everyone waited in heavy silence.

Now, Pearl began to sing in the sweetest voice Chance had ever heard. As requested, she began with "Red River Valley":

"From this valley, they say you are leaving,
When you go, may your darling go, too?
Would you leave her behind unprotected,
When she loves none other but you..."

Chance swallowed hard. He wanted to leave but he was mesmerized.

She sang other songs the crowd requested, but her last song touched everyone. She concluded with "Amazing Grace."

At the end of the hymn, many were teary-eyed.

Chance, himself, had to sniff. The applause was loud and lingering. Unable to handle how he felt, he retreated to the lobby with Truman on his heels. Two hotel men guarding the exit let them pass.

Years of repressing his feelings had just exploded inside of him.

"Chance, are you all right?"

"Yeah."

"Let's wait for her to come out, and..."

"Tell her she was a good singer." Chance headed for the front door exit just as the lounge lights were brightened behind them.

"Marshal!" a sweet voice called after them.

Stopped in his tracks, forced to be polite, Chance took a deep breath. Slowly, he turned as Pearl and Truman came over to him. She looked so beautiful, he wanted to run.

The hotel men continued to block the lounge exit for her protection.

Hat in hand, Chance could only stare at her lovely face. The lace on her collar had parted at one edge. He had an urge to reach out and fix it into place.

"I'm leaving tomorrow," she said directly to Chance. "I just wanted to say goodbye. And I hope you come to East Ridge, sometime."

"He will," Truman said with a grin.

She came closer to Chance and smiled up at him as his heart went crazy.

"I'm not mad at you anymore," she said, her eyes shining as if teary.

Chance had no voice. He could only nod, bow slightly, spin, and charge out the door.

Pearl stared after him. "He doesn't like me."

Truman chuckled. "Are you kidding?"

She flushed. "If only…"

*　　*　　*　　*

Later that night in his lonely room at the Stockman's Hotel, Chance downed another glass of water to put out the fire from the chili.

Her musical voice kept ringing softly in his ears. At the same time, he knew for certain she was married, out of reach, and would ever remain a fantasy.

He told himself she had only reminded him that he was a lonely man. He had often prayed he would someday marry and have a family, grow old on the front porch with a glass of lemonade and a ranch spread out before him.

He convinced himself that Pearl had been an unavailable reflection of that need. He also knew he would be alone as long as he lived his life trapped in bitter memory.

He would have a restless night.

*   *   *   *

In early August, 1898, Pearl Hart was still at East Ridge, where the weather ranged from hot and dry to stormy with hail and rain. She enjoyed her simple cabin when not working. She slept well because she thought her husband's only letter said he would be in the army a long while. Unknown to her, he would soon muster out as the war in Cuba was ending.

She enjoyed working in Lester's restaurant because the miners loved her being there. It was hard work but made her strangely proud. Most of them treated her as family. She was not used to such kind treatment. When she did sing at a mealtime, they could not cheer her enough, and sometimes even left a large gratuity.

Every extra dollar she made, she had Lester turn into a bank draft, and she would then send it to her brother. His letters said the first operation had failed, so they were not rushing into the next. Pearl did a lot of praying.

Joe Boot had disappeared some time ago, and she found she missed his company, even if he was a dandy. She had never even considered being unfaithful to her nasty husband, but she did get lonely, and Joe could be entertaining.

Truman did stop by once and had brought her a bit of joy. He seemed to look at her like a daughter, something she had never experienced, as her father had disapproved of her for most of her life.

It would have also pleased her if Chance had ridden by, but he had not. He was the kind of man she could have dearly loved as a husband, someone just and strong, a man she realized she already looked up to and admired.

*   *   *   *

Meanwhile, in the town of Florence, seat of Pinal County, Arizona Territory, on a clear but windy morning, a posse of four mounted men waited in the street. They were prepared with bedrolls, canteens and possible sacks. A mule on lead was heavy laden.

The posse had been formed in a hurry. They would be paid for their time and use of their horses. None were on a particular mission, as they were working ranch hands who could use the extra pay.

Sheriff Truman came out of his office and onto the boardwalk. He was dressed to ride with his long coat and carried a Winchester repeater. Short guns were good close up, but a posse always expected to run into rifle fire.

Truman was glad to see Chance riding up the street and dismounting at the rail in front of the building. Chance's saddle carried his bedroll, possibles, and canteen.

They shook hands. Male onlookers stood back but didn't volunteer.

Chance looked around. "You sent word there was trouble."

"Yeah, and it may take us out of my jurisdiction. That's why we need you."

With a nod, Chance waited as they moved into the shade, out of earshot, and Truman continued.

"Last night, there was a break-in near midnight at the express office. Guard heard a noise and looked out into the alley. He was hit from behind and dragged inside. They beat him so bad, they thought he was dead. He said they stank to high Heaven, as if they hadn't washed in weeks."

Truman paused to adjust his gunbelt before continuing.

"They were masked, but one's face cover slid down as the safe was being cleaned out. It was loaded with payrolls for the mines and railroads. They took a fortune in gold and currency. Other witnesses reported seeing maybe seven or eight strangers riding out in a real hurry."

"Did the guard know who the man was, the face he saw?"

"Yeah, from posters I showed him. It was Trey Boxer, not heard of since he and his gang busted out down in Mexico. The others could have been his four sons and a couple more hard cases."

Chance turned hot with bitter memory. Yes, he had seen the Boxers' faces on recent posters. Older now and bearded, they were still recognizable. He was certain of one thing: not one of them would connect a skinny little kid with the big, tall lawman. Not even Trey Boxer.

He walked toward his buckskin with Truman at his side. The sheriff claimed his own mount, a roan gelding, on a nearby hitching rail. They both freed their horses and mounted to join the posse.

"They headed north," Truman said as he slid his rifle into the scabbard. "Across the desert."

"They'll see us coming from miles away." Chance tugged at his hat brim.

"Not to worry." Truman nodded to an aging Indian on a sorrel. "We got old Tom with us. He can track a roadrunner in a sand storm."

"I'd like to see that."

"He thinks they're likely headed for that ridge formation, other side of Coyote Creek. The one they call the Beehive."

"Caves and canyons," Chance said. "Ripe for ambush."

Tom, a middle-aged Ute wearing ranch clothes and a red hatband on his Stetson, rode over to join the posse. It would be seven riding for the law, trailing seven or eight outlaws.

Truman started riding with a wave to the men to follow.

As they continued due north, they watched dark clouds threaten the distant mountains ahead of them. Red rocks, salt brush, and sage could hide a rattlesnake at any turn. Prairie dogs barked at their intrusion.

The outlaws had left signs only Tom could find as they crossed the now windy desert with blowing sand.

A red-tailed hawk sailed above in the sky, then darted out of sight.

Tall, soaptree yucca greeted them with a few remaining yellow blossoms. Leafless palo verde with green bark and white flowers of the prickle poppy could be seen. Mesquite with spiny twigs was all around.

The sudden sight of a dozen racing pronghorn antelope crossing their path far ahead was welcome but startled the horses. The tan and white critters hurried west and soon vanished in the tall brush and dwarf junipers.

Riding continually north, the posse avoided unfriendly cholla and a few prickly pear cactus still showing yellow blooms. Sagebrush, silver and sometimes aromatic, was everywhere. When night fell, the hot sun gave way to a chill in their camp.

They needed the rest, but few could sleep, knowing a fight was ahead.

*   *   *   *

When Truman, Chance, and the posse sighted the distant beehive ridges, it was late afternoon the next day. Dark clouds had moved overhead, shutting out the sun. A bitter wind was already tearing at them.

The ridge cluster was rocky, many miles wide, and towering with caves, narrow passages, brush, and stunt juniper. The landscape was formidable.

They knew they were heading for a possible trap.

CHAPTER FIVE

It was mid-afternoon, overcast and still threatening rain when they neared the Beehive. In the far north were the mountains with silver diggings, crested with fresh snow while dark clouds hovered.

At the forty-foot-wide mouth of one of the many canyons, deep in the rocky terrain of the ridge with its odd formations, Tom had found a trail for the posse to follow.

The lawmen clustered on horseback near the red-tinted canyon entrance. They could see up along barren high walls, yellow in streaks, reaching one hundred feet high on both sides, marching toward a narrow but brief turn in the canyon path. It was impossible to see beyond the immediate imposing walls.

Truman gestured. "Tom says this canyon is pretty short and leads into open country. That narrow pass is only wide enough for single file. It's maybe ten yards in before it straightens out and is wide open again. That's where the east wall disappears. He says the west wall continues but is only half as high and has easy access from the rear, so if they're waiting for us, it'll be there on our left as we ride in."

"Can you get around behind them?"

Truman nods. "Won't be easy, but Tom says we can."

"I'll ride in just far enough to let 'em know I'm there to whet their appetite."

"Don't take any chances. Give us maybe half an hour." Truman tugged at his hat.

There was a sudden rising of the wind, whistling through the pass.

Chance held out his hand to catch some rain drops.

Truman nodded. "Yeah, we're going to get wet."

"And so are they."

The sky darkened even more. Light rain began to fall.

Chance waited as the posse moved west to find a spot to make their way into the honeycombed terrain. It might not be easy, but they would try to sneak up on the outlaws from behind.

Using himself as bait, Chance rode north up the canyon, rifle in hand. Sweat formed on his face. He pushed his hat back and kept riding. It was not likely he could be seen because of the high walls, but once he went through the pass, he knew he would be in the open and they'd be waiting on the left wall.

He neared the sharp turn in the canyon and dismounted. He led his horse into the narrow passage. Rain was gently falling.

Chance was not ready to tell his secrets, not even to Trey Boxer. He had carried the truth so long, just the revelation itself would be too painful to speak. He had held to his adoptive father's teachings and would do his duty, but bitterness cropped up at Chance's every thought.

Peering out through the turn into the wider path ahead, he

could see the east wall had fallen away to open space on his right.

To the west and left of him, there was still a steep wall up to eighty feet high. It was heavy with rocks and brush and backed up to even rougher terrain. It reached several hundred yards ahead before it dropped off and gave way to open, rolling ground.

On the height of the wall on his left, he caught a glimpse of a rifle barrel.

Rain was now steady, heavier. The icy wind swept it in all directions.

Chance backed away and remained out of sight. He let time pass so that the posse could get up behind them, likely now on foot. He pulled his rifle, put his hat on the end of it, ready to stick it out in the gang's view but was in no hurry. With his buckskin behind him, he waited.

Eight grimy, unwashed men on the west wall with ample cover from brush and rocks, were spread out and cussing at the rain. They wore rough outfits, some picked up in Mexico, making them appear foreign. Behind them, heavy terrain, but to the north, the wall soon dropped down to a hollow where the horses, saddles hung with loot in gunny sacks, remained hidden. Slickers were still tied with bedrolls.

The hollow where the horses waited opened along the north side of the rocky terrain. From there, they could ride west unseen.

The bushwhackers huddled high on the wall, ready for ambush.

The leader was Trey Boxer, in his late sixties with ratty grey hair and beard, beady brown eyes, and a sinister face. To his right were his four sons, in their thirties and forties, raunchy, bearded, and deadly. Rip was the oldest, followed by Rory, Rafe, and Rufus. They hunched down in the rocks and brush.

To his sons' far right were fierce, ugly killers and brothers, Thad Mason, in his fifties, and his younger brother Carl, in his forties, both with black hair, mustaches, and dark brown eyes. They were gang members of long-time association and were also distant kin.

Way back to the north of the wall, Joe Boot, Trey's nephew and cousin to Trey's sons, hunched down. He looked behind him and down some hundred feet to where the horses stood. Beyond the hollow's half circle was open country.

Trey Boxer cussed the rain until it became lighter again. He figured he scared it off. He was uncomfortable in the rocks, scratched his beard, aimed his rifle. No target. High rocks blocked the view of the canyon entrance. They could only await anyone foolish enough to come through the narrow slot.

Sunlight suddenly broke through the fast moving clouds.

"They weren't that far behind us," Trey growled. "Where the devil are they?"

They heard their horses whinny and snort down in the hollow.

Trey called out in a low, gruff voice and signaled to his nephew. "Joe, get back down there and keep the horses quiet."

"He should be over here. He's our best shot," Rip said.

"And the clumsiest." Trey muttered. "But I already lost my only brother. I don't want to lose his only kid."

Joe turned, looked at the horses a long way down below him. He didn't mind getting down there with the loot hung on the saddles. With a posse closing in, he might need an escape route. Although he was willing to kill, he was secretly afraid of being shot himself because, hey, it might hurt like the devil.

Joe started down, stumbled on loose rock, sailed, and landed hard on his rump, then slid downhill at great speed. Frantic, he grabbed at brush and whined at the stickers.

"Yikes!"

He crashed down by the startled horses and rolled against more brush.

Up above, having seen Joe disappear into the hollow, Trey shook his head and chuckled. "Darn kid. Trips over his own boots."

Up on the wall, the Boxers kept watching the narrow opening in the pass, hoping and waiting.

"How do we know Donovan's even with the posse?" Thad Mason called over to Trey in a low voice. "We could have been halfway to California by now."

Trey's son Rip, hunched down near him, responded. "Joe saw him in Phoenix and said he's a big man, just like the one we had sight of, trailing us with the posse."

"You know, we lost kin in that bank robbery, same as you," Thad said. "But killing another Donovan isn't worth ending up in Yuma."

Rip glared at him. "The ranger we shot was a couple hundred miles away when our uncle Randy was killed. So, now we figure we got the right Donovan. And our pa wants him dead."

Trey was annoyed at the argument. "Just keep your voices down."

Thad quieted only because, like all of them, he was afraid of Trey.

Unseen by the Boxers, down in the remuda, Joe recovered

from his fall and stood up. He was able to see Trey's hat way above on the wall but no other sign of his kin.

The horses were slow to settle back down. He could see past them, out of the hollow and into the open. He knew the silver diggings were in the mountains to the far north, and he'd often thought of getting rich up there. Anywhere there were mines, there would be gambling halls, and he could have a fistful of dollars in no time.

He didn't like his uncle too much, and his cousins were often annoying. Yes, he was here to avenge his father's death, but he also knew Trey would take care of that without his help, and there was an awful lot of money on those saddles.

In the canyon, stuck in the narrow turn in the pass, Chance stood by his horse with his rifle. His hat dangled on the end of the barrel. Granite rose high around him. Rain dribbled on him through the narrow crack above.

Up there on the wall was Trey Boxer, a man Chance hated, and for good reason. But he forced himself to swallow his anger, do his duty, and trust in the Lord. He had to honor his late adoptive father, no matter how much it hurt.

He had to assume the posse was already close behind the outlaws, so he needed to distract the gang, and he poked his rifle and hat out into view.

Immediately, Trey Boxer fired. The hat spun and fell back near Chance's feet.

Chance recovered his hat and veered out just enough to fire at another flash on the ridge as a shot hit the wall near him. His return fire hit Trey across the top of his head, sending his hat flying and leaving a bloody crease in his grey hair.

Trey yelped and ducked down.

Chance called from the turn in the canyon. "Throw down your weapons. You're all under arrest for robbery and attempted murder."

Trey Boxer burned with anger. "That you, Donovan?"

Chance didn't respond.

When he had shot at Trey, Chance had spotted the Mason brothers over to the left. He leaned out with his rifle just as Carl showed himself as he fired. Chance fired back, fast and sure, hitting Carl in the right shoulder. Carl crashed back into the rocks as his brother Thad cussed out loud and returned fire.

Chance remained unhurt and under cover.

The outlaws huddled down now and waited for Chance to appear. The sky darkened. Fierce wind and rain returned with small hail, pounding like bullets, but only for a few minutes. Then it was only the wind, with bits of sunlight shooting through the fast moving clouds.

As the storm cleared, Truman's posse moved slowly on foot from the west along the rise through red chunks of terrain and dark green junipers. They advanced within thirty feet of where the outlaws, their backs to the posse, hovered over the canyon.

In position with his rifle, Truman yelled, "Get your hands up!"

Trey spun to fire. Truman's shot whistled past his bloodied head.

The posse, closing in, was still under cover, but the outlaws were not.

"Now!" Truman shouted.

Trey, blood running down by his left ear from under his

recovered hat, dropped his rifle, as did his sons. The wounded Carl and his brother Thad also gave up and lifted their hands in the air.

Below in the canyon, Chance kept his rifle on them, but he was going to hang back and let Truman handle it. He felt shaken by the wounding of Trey, but he would keep his word to his Ranger father.

Out of sight of the posse and down with the horses in the hollow, Joe could see up on the wall where his uncle had surrendered with his hands up. He couldn't see the others but he knew they were all being arrested.

He had to make a run for it, but not without some of the loot.

Although the rain had stopped, the fierce wind made the animals nervous, and they shied away from him while tethered.

Sacks of money hung from the saddles on the skittish horses, with a big one on Trey's nervous gelding, which reared, spun, and knocked Joe down.

Joe jumped up and started to take another grab for the money on other horses but fumbled as they danced around. He looked up, saw no one but heard a lot of cussing. He finally grabbed the money sack off the horn of Trey's horse. Then, he saw a gold chain dangling from his uncle's saddle bag. He knew it was the gold watch they had taken from a dead ranger. He could gamble it away or sell it. He fished it out as the horse spun again and knocked him against the cliff wall.

Joe recovered, went to his own horse, caught up the reins, and managed to mount with the money sack and gold watch. As much as he wanted more, he was terrified he would be seen. He couldn't even chance leading away the other horses.

Joe rode from the hollow, west, and close to the side of the high terrain on his left, leaving no obvious prints on the rocky ground. He soon found safety and cover in a distant hollow in the wall where he could hide until it was over. If he rode into the open now, he would likely be seen.

He would lay low until they were gone, for certain, then head north for the diggings.

Despite the rain having stopped, the wind was relentless.

Joe huddled down next to his horse. He tried to count some of the money in the sack, but the wind grabbed at it, so he tied it back up and held it against him.

The robbery of the express office in Florence had been exhilarating but scary, and he would be glad to get back to the tables and his more peaceful way of life.

It was on his mind to go to East Ridge and tie up with Pearl. She could be fun, but he was even more interested in using her to annoy the marshal.

In the constant wind, the outlaws on the wall had dropped their rifles, knives, and gunbelts. They had lost any advantage, and Trey was so furious, he ignored the blood dribbling down his left temple from his head wound. He owed Donovan for that, and a lot more.

The posse tied the outlaws' hands behind them, except for the wounded Carl. The prisoners were grumbling, hungry, wet, and angry.

One of the posse, further north on the wall, spotted the outlaws' horses, but long after Joe was out of sight. He called to Truman. "I got their horses."

"Bring 'em around and meet us out front," Truman shouted

and sent one more of the posse to assist.

A short while later, the prisoners, now in the open by a chip campfire, faced the south end of the canyon in bright sunlight as the clouds passed.

At that moment, the two posse members, riding two of the outlaws' horses and leading the others, also came out of the canyon.

Now, they saw Chance follow them as he rode out into the open.

Trey snarled at the sight of him, hating him for the death of Trey's brother, unaware Chance had reason to take his own revenge on Trey.

Truman waved to Chance, who held back near the canyon.

Then the sheriff turned to Trey. "Trey Boxer, isn't it? You didn't kill that guard."

"Yeah?" Trey snapped. "Too bad."

"And he got a good look at your pretty face."

"Yeah, well, I won't forget yours," Trey snarled.

Truman wasn't afraid of him. "By the time you get out of Yuma, I'll be retired and fishing on some mountain stream, a long way from here."

Trey sneered and blinked as blood neared his left eye.

That night under a clear sky, the weary posse settled by campfires south of the canyon entrance. With money recovered, and the wounded Trey and Carl treated, there was temporary calm. No one knew Joe had been there and had taken off with some of the loot.

Chance kept away from the prisoners and everyone but Truman.

Coffee and beans and hard tack was shared with the prisoners.

Early morning of the next day, they broke camp, and all were once again mounted for the long ride back to Florence.

Out of earshot of the others, Chance rode over to Truman.

"You don't need me now," he said. "I'm turning them over to your authority."

Truman agreed. "Where you headed?"

"Gila City. Some trouble on the border down there."

"Well, don't worry, we'll take good care of the Boxers."

"I hope that's the end of it."

"Texas will want them, and so will Mexico, but we get first crack. And I figure they're going to end their days in Yuma, if I can help it."

"Good luck."

"You know, when you get done at the border, it wouldn't hurt you to take a ride back up north to East Ridge and check on Pearl."

"If I get up that way," Chance hedged.

"She's had a hard life."

"I'm aware of that."

"So?"

"Nothing I can do about it."

As he rode south and away from the posse and prisoners, he struggled with leaving Trey in other hands. But he was needed at the border and tried to concentrate on that.

He rode south for a time and then west toward the sunset.

The wind had died down and the desert was more friendly than usual, although at nightfall, it would turn cold. Now, he saw a black turkey buzzard riding the wind ahead of him. He leaned forward to stroke his buckskin's neck.

"Don't worry, Sam, it's not our turn."

As he rode, he tried not to think back. It should have satisfied him that Trey Boxer was going back to prison, but it didn't. There was too much history between them.

'Okay, Dad, I did my duty and that's all, but it sure wasn't easy.'

CHAPTER SIX

In early September of 1898, high in the mountains, East Ridge Mining Camp was surrounded by towering ponderosa and pointed crowns of lower Douglas firs, along with shiny green aspens and stunted junipers. Rocky Mountain white oak, short with shiny leaves, and patches of thorny shrubs, some with berries, decorated the landscape.

The ridges rising above the pines were crimson and yellow. Mines were dug into their bases, often with machinery pumping water.

Most days were sunny but when the rains came, they were sudden and violent, with flash floods and tents sailing off with them.

East Ridge was a typical boomtown with quick buildings, shacks, and tents, and messy mining camp equipment with empty crates in stacks near the livery. Clustered were saloons, dining halls, a general store, with no law present.

There were no boardwalks, only stony paths.

Lester's Restaurant was mostly outdoors with long tables and benches shaded by oaks and pines, along with short junipers and brush. Set by itself to the west side of the street, it was in view of the other side across an open field that led to where there were competitive food places, stores, and saloons.

It had been raining that morning but had cleared to new sunlight. Pearl, the very popular cook, came out for some fresh air after the breakfast run. Miners filled the outdoor tables and many would stay for the noon meal. They could not get enough of her cooking.

A young man in a long white apron was serving them with the help of a chubby waitress. The aroma from the kitchen was captivating.

The mine workers, ever weary, were all in love with Pearl.

Old timers were fatherly, and one, smiling under his drooping handlebar mustache, stopped her when she came by his table. He had twinkling eyes.

"Miss Pearl, when I was a young feller and trailing cattle north from Texas to the Kansas railroads, I thought there was nothing better than waking up at the crack of dawn to the smell of bacon sizzling in the cocinero's pan."

Pearl was touched and speechless as he continued.

"But what comes out of your kitchen, all those delicious smells, just like our mothers' home cooking, that warms a man's heart and stays with him all day. And this old timer thanks you for bringing a touch of family to us."

Pearl had tears in her eyes as she leaned over, pushed his grimy hat back, and kissed his sun-dried cheek.

The old timer's face turned pink, but his eyes were wet.

Unable to stop her tears, Pearl excused herself, returning to hide in the kitchen.

The miner's kindness had filled her with joy and gratitude. It was a new and wonderful feeling.

After the afternoon meal ended, Pearl shed her apron and wandered toward the water trough and hitching rail on the same side of the street. Wearing a blue gingham dress with the usual high collar and long sleeves, she looked prim and proper. But there was a dark bruise on her left cheek.

She glanced around behind her at her lone cabin, then turned to stare across at the other side where a lot of horses near the saloons indicated gambling was ongoing. She could hear someone sawing boards, probably building another shack or saloon.

Alone on the stony path, she watched an oncoming rider from the west.

She backed away as Joe Boot reined up at the rail. Ever the dandy in his gambling wear, he tipped his hat. He looked harmless, so she smiled and turned her back, about to go to her cabin.

"You look beautiful," he said, causing her to turn around again.

Long since having sent some of the express money to a friend to look for ways to get his uncle and cousins out of prison, and having gambled away the rest of it at West Ridge Diggings, Joe was here for a fresh start. He still had the gold watch and a few winnings. He had also won a mining claim, but so far, had found it barren.

He stepped down, his left hand hiding a bouquet of yellow, purple, and white wild flowers behind his back. He came closer even as she backed away.

"I'm Joe Boot. And I saw you in Phoenix. I heard you sing."

"And?"

"You have a right pretty voice."

"And you have a funny name."

He liked her comeback. "Oh, it's really a stage name, but I just kind of adopted it."

"Stage?"

"I do trick shot and fast draw." He bowed. "I'm famous."

"I'll bet."

Pearl smiled because she desperately needed the attention. Her husband had mustered out, shown up last night, stolen all she had saved, and had left at the break of dawn for parts unknown. Her long sleeves hid the bruises on her left arm.

"Yeah," Joe continued with a grin, "and I saw the marshal rescue you. Picked you right out of the mud."

And, he thought, *you might be just the bait we need to get Donovan.*

What he wanted, until his uncle and cousins escaped prison, was to be so entangled with Pearl that Chance would be jealous and off guard. There could be some opportunity to take Chance down, if Joe had the courage. As ever, his only hesitation was that he didn't want to be the one who got shot. Even though he was likely the fastest gun ever, he was still afraid of pain.

Joe bowed slightly as Pearl backed away in the sunlight.

"You're about the prettiest little lady I've ever seen."

His jovial manner made it easy for a comeback. "You all sound alike. All hat and no cattle."

She started back toward the café as he kept at her side.

"You're a sassy one," he said.

He hurried in front of her, turned to offer the flowers.

She stopped, startled, impressed, softening. She took the bouquet, held them close and sniffed them. "Thank you. Where did you find these?"

"Up on the ridge. Want to ride up there?"

She continued to walk. "I'm married."

"He put that mark on your face?" he asked, keeping at her side.

She stopped, nodded, desperately in need of a friend.

"He was here last night, but he's gone now. Back to Phoenix. Until he runs out of the money he took from me."

Joe hooked his thumbs in his gunbelt in a cocky stance. "Let me teach him a lesson."

She shook her head, long ago having given up on any chance of freedom.

Joe saw an easy opening. "So, you're going to pine away like an old maid? Let men keep you in your place? Is that it? Or you could have a mighty fine time with a real nice feller. Why, I'd even take you on a picnic up to the top of the ridge. If you ain't scared."

"Of you? Not likely."

Finding him charming, harmless and carefree, she agreed, not knowing he was really a member of the deadly Boxer Gang.

High up in the ridges on the following weekend, Joe and Pearl were seated on a blanket on a mostly dry, grassy height near pines and aspen. Clouds hovered but the sun had broken through. There was no breeze, only the warm sunlight.

They were having a picnic and enjoying the view of the snow caps further north ahead of them, and the red desert far behind them to the south. Their horses were nearby.

Pearl had ridden a man's saddle with no difficulty. She wore a navy blue, split riding skirt, a white blouse with high collar, and a blue jacket. She looked lovely with a matching blue ribbon under her chin, holding her wide brimmed hat.

Joe Boot showed great admiration. If he had to use her to annoy Chance, there was no reason he shouldn't enjoy himself, too. She was feisty but sweet and very pretty. She was the kind of woman most men dream of, someone to share their life, side by side. Even Joe could see her this way, but not yet.

Wonderful flowers abounded on the ridge. Pearl had some in a bouquet at her side.

She had prepared fried chicken, biscuits and a salad, along with lemonade.

When they had eaten, he patted his stomach to show his satisfaction.

He stood up as she leaned over to clear the leftovers and put them in the basket. He stretched, showing off his handsome physique. Then he sat down again and adjusted his hat as he asked a question, trying to win her confidence.

"What was it like, growing up in Canada?"

"Lonely. My family and church were very strict. I was sent to a Christian boarding school, and it was the same. Spent half my time staring out the window." She smiled and shook her head. "I had this dream of the Wild West. I used to hide dime novels in my school books. Even in the choir, I... well..." She paused to reflect, shook her head. "We went as a class to see *King Lear* on stage, and there was Fred in the chorus. It wasn't long before he found me. I just fell for him and his big promises."

She looked sad and longing for a change.

"Stick with me, little lady," Joe said. "My old grandfather is leaving me a fortune one of these days. Up in Denver."

"Is that where you're from?"

"Yep."

"Is that why you don't work?"

"That, and I'm *very* lucky at cards."

"Fred told me the same, but he gambled away every cent we had." She shook her head. "All my fault, of course. Sometimes, he would hit me. I sang for money so he would stop."

"And all this time, he didn't realize the real treasure was you."

Flattered, she looked away.

He took her hand, and pulled her to her feet. "You can trust me, Pearl."

He caressed her face with the tip of his finger. Lonely, miserable, trapped in a bad marriage, and now courted so gently, she was transfixed.

"He didn't know how lucky he was."

Joe bent his head, tried to kiss her. Pearl broke free and backed away. She sank back down on the picnic blanket. Badly shaken, she realized how vulnerable she was, and it was a little frightening.

Joe didn't push his luck and changed his tact. "Did I tell you I was a star in the wild west shows? Everyone thought I was the champion of the whole frontier."

She shook her head with a grin.

"Watch this, Pearl."

Standing with feet apart, he was ready with his right hand. With great showmanship, he drew his six-gun, so fast she didn't see him draw. He twirled it in the road agent's spin. Holstered it fast and slick.

Pearl, amazed, appreciated his showing off. "I didn't see your hand move."

Joe grinned. "Fastest draw in the West. They tried to time me, but I beat the clock."

Glad for the distraction and a great show, she sat back with a big smile.

Joe proceeded to show his marksmanship, fast drew, fired, hit nearby targets until his six-gun was empty.

Pearl was suitably impressed as he reloaded.

Joe continued to put on a real show for her. One last fast draw. He really put his stance to work and pointed to a tree limb, far off.

Joe hunched down, hand near his holster, grabbed at his weapon to draw.

His six-gun fired in the holster, hit his right boot, and penetrated at the big toe.

"Yikes!" Joe hopped around in pain.

Pearl tried not to laugh, but failed. "Is that why they call you Joe Boot?"

Joe sat down and yanked off his boot, scowling. The bullet had just scraped his big toe. It was sore but not bleeding.

Pearl covered her mouth with her hand but giggled.

Joe glared at her, then had a foolish grin. "Okay, so I was showing off, but you got no polish and no sympathy."

Pearl smiled at the half compliment. '*I need your company,*' she thought. '*You're cheerful, and funny. And I'm so lonely. I have a husband who hits me and takes my money, and the law says that's okay. And the man I could truly love, that big oak tree of a marshal, I can never have. So, keep me laughing, Joe, please.*'

*   *   *   *

Weeks later at the East Ridge mining camp, Pearl left work at Lester's restaurant late in the day. It had stopped raining and was sunny and warm, but off the stone paths, it was still muddy with standing water. She wore a jacket over her green dress but no protection for her long, lustrous hair.

She paused and watched as Joe Boot approached on foot.

"Another letter from my brother," she said, shaking her head.

"That's tough, I know. And I'm sorry my claim didn't work out. All our digging for nothing."

"We tried."

"It was worth it to see you in boys' britches. I'm saving them."

She looked at her bruised hands. "I'm done with shoveling dirt."

He didn't mention the other plans he had for her, like trying to make a certain lawman lose his edge.

"My mother will think I've forsaken her," she said.

"No, Pearl, you do everything you can. What about your church up there? Doesn't it have a way to help?"

"I'm afraid to ask."

"Why?"

"All those bad stories about me."

"I'm sure your ma knows they're lies, but where's your pa in all this?"

"He disappeared years ago." She withdrew her hand. "What about your mother and father?"

Joe shrugged. "Lost her when I was ten. And then my father in Texas, five years ago."

"I'm so sorry. No brothers and sisters?"

"Not a one. Just a few kinfolk."

She stood up with him.

They walked a short distance away from the restaurant and stopped near the watering trough and hitching rail, which faced the muddy street.

Coming south along the way was Chance Donovan. He looked tall and handsome in the saddle. Pearl tried not to swoon at sight of him. Joe was instantly jealous, not only because of Pearl, but the lawman struck such a grand figure. His star caught the sunlight and he looked like a vision right out of an old west painting.

Joe made a face. "What's he doing here?"

"Maybe he's worried about me," she said, knowing it was wishful thinking.

"Tell 'im I got the job now."

She ignored Joe's claim. All she could think about was that this was the first time Chance had come to East Ridge.

Chance rode up, reined to a halt by the trough to let his horse drink. He tipped his hat, leaned on the pommel, studied her and Joe Boot. Chance had never thought he'd ever be in a spot where he was yearning for an impossible love. But there she was. Pretty as a picture and with a look in her eyes that said she liked him, too.

"You have such a beautiful horse," she said. "What's his name?"

"Sam."

"After Sam Houston?" she asked.

"How did you know?"

"You were a Texas Ranger. It just... fits."

Chance nodded his thanks.

Pearl smiled up at him and gestured. "Marshal, this is my friend, Joe Boot."

Joe looked cocky. "More than a friend."

Pearl glared at Joe. "You can wish."

Chance looked Joe Boot over with instant distaste and addressed him. "Haven't I seen you somewhere?"

"Not unless you've seen me on stage. I'm a fast draw. Trick shot."

Joe tried to look taller, more dangerous.

Chance then ignored him, turned to gaze down at Pearl. "Just checking to see if you're all right."

Joe Boot swelled up, moved over to her side. He knew that Chance really was sweet on her, because it was so obvious. This was an opportunity to needle him. "I'm taking care of her."

"No, Joe, you're not," she said, chin up. "I can take care of myself."

Joe hung back as she smiled up at Chance, who now said why he had really ridden all the way to East Ridge.

"Fred Hart is in jail in Florence," Chance told her. "Saloon brawl over a card game."

"For how long?" she asked, startled.

"Thirty days. He's only served a week."

Pearl felt a mix of gratitude and misery. It was the middle of September, 1898, and she would count the days during which she would be temporarily free of Fred's visits and she could save money to send to Canada for her mother.

Chance tipped his hat without cracking a smile and turned his buckskin to ride down the street, heading out of town to the south.

Pearl rested her hand on her bosom as if to contain what she felt. It seemed Chance didn't want to hear her sing. He'd only came as a lawman to deliver news and now was gone. That was painful for her.

Joe was disgruntled. "Why didn't you tell him you needed money for your ma? And how your old man stole all you had saved when he was here? Donovan would have given you all you need."

"I'd never, ever ask him."

Joe glared after Chance until he rode past buildings and out of sight. Joe was jealous and didn't like the way her gaze followed the lawman's departure. Just the same, she would be his bait. Joe didn't want the man who shot his father to ever be happy with this beautiful woman, but first came revenge.

Joe turned to Pearl. "You sweet on him?"

"I'm not sweet on anybody. Not even you."

"So, you're just using me," he said with a grin.

Joe and Pearl turned back toward the restaurant as Chance had now ridden out of sight. A rising wind tossed her hair about her face.

Joe wanted Chance dead, but he was waiting for his uncle and cousins to get out of prison. They were in for twenty years for the Florence robbery, but he knew that wouldn't keep them inside for long. He had given away a lot of money from the express robbery, all to arrange it.

Meanwhile, taunting Chance with Pearl was his happy way to pass the time.

Pearl tried not to think about Chance. She had told herself there would never be a day that she would be in his arms. She did feel that he liked her, but it had to end there. It was a relief, at least, to learn her abusive husband was in jail for a time.

All she had now in her life was Joe Boot, an amusing friend. They had dug in his mining claim for weeks, but they had found nothing of value like silver, only traces of copper. Just the same, she was grateful for the distracting effort.

CHAPTER SEVEN

On a Thursday afternoon in bright sunlight, Lester walked Pearl home from the restaurant. He wore a straw hat and striped shirt. Pearl looked lovely in a blue dress with her hair tied back. They were on the stone path leading to where the watering trough marked the way to her cabin.

"Pearl, if Joe Boot bothers you at home, fire off your pistol and I'll send some of my boys."

"He's gone back to the Last Chance," she said.

"Last I saw, he was lit up like a candle. And sure smelled of whiskey."

"He's always been such a gentleman. I've never seen him this way. Not as long as I've known him. But he's been losing money at cards and that's a new thing for him. I don't know if he's tangled with a card sharp, but he's lost his edge. And then, he received a letter that upset him."

"Letter? Who from?"

"I don't know, but he said he needed money to get his uncle out of prison."

They stopped and turned to see Chance riding in from the north.

Pearl's heart skipped a beat at her joy in seeing the lawman again.

"You got a thing for him," Lester observed.

"It's just wishful thinking."

Chance rode over to the trough and since Sam was still cool from the leisurely walk, let him drink. Seeing Pearl's smile, Chance tipped his hat to her and nodded to Lester.

"Good to see you," Lester said to him. "We got no preacher here, but if you're sticking around, Silas Cain, he owns the Last Chance Saloon across the way, and he's starting his own brand of church services. He's heard our Pearl sing, so he's going to set it up at his place this Sunday morning. He and I, we'll do some Bible reading. She'll sing some solos, then lead the miners in a few hymns."

Chance was impressed. "Sounds like a fine idea, but I have to get back for a trial in Florence. It may go on for a week."

Lester turned to the weary Pearl. "You go on home and get some rest, Pearl. I'll keep an eye out so no one bothers you."

She smiled so beautifully at Chance, he felt his own heart skip a beat.

She squeezed Lester's arm and headed west on the path to her cabin.

After she was safely inside, Lester turned to Chance, who had now stepped down.

Lester talked quietly. "Joe Boot is drunk as a skunk. He was over at the restaurant, ranting and raving and scaring her. Asking her for money."

Chance felt anger but didn't respond.

"Seems he's losing at cards for the first time ever. She said he was also upset about a letter he received."

Immediately alert, Chance grimaced. "What letter? Who from?"

"She doesn't know. He told her he needed money to get his uncle out of prison."

"Where is he?"

"Went back across to the Last Chance Saloon."

Chance tugged at his hat brim and was about to turn when Lester stopped him.

"Something else, Chance. He's so desperate for money, he tried to sell me a watch. A gold watch."

"What? Did you see it?"

"Yeah, but I couldn't get my hands on it. I told him no, but I got to thinking how you once said your father's was stolen. I was going to go over there and buy it, but now you're here."

"Yes, I'm here."

"Take it easy, Chance. There are a lot of gold watches."

Chance mounted and rode across the street to the front of the saloon where a dozen horses were at the rail.

Inside the Silver Dollar Saloon, a dozen miners were at the poker tables. Most of them wore dirty clothes and looked as if they hadn't had a bath or a shave in weeks. Along with whiskey and smoke, it wasn't the most pleasant atmosphere.

There were only two women who worked in the saloon, but both were missing and probably busy. There was a long walnut bar, which was just inside the entrance.

As Chance entered the noisy, smoky saloon, he noticed an empty seat at one of the tables. He spotted the red bearded Colby, a known card sharp in his forties who dressed like a ranch hand to catch the other players off guard, and who Chance had thrown in jail more than once. He felt no urge to warn Joe Boot.

Chance moved to the walnut bar and looked over to his right. The balding barkeep was arguing with Joe, who was leaning on the bar and drinking.

Unaware of Chance, Joe pulled the gold watch out of his coat pocket and offered it. He slurred his words. "I need twenty dollars, real quick. I'm sitting on a straight flush."

The barkeep examined it, but shook his head. "Already got three of these on hold. Maybe I can give you five dollars, if the boss okays it."

Chance, looking grim, moved closer to Joe. "Maybe I can make an offer."

Joe Boot recognized the lawman but was too intoxicated and desperate to think straight, not even remembering where he got the watch in his drunken state. He slid it over to him.

Chance opened the back of the watch and saw the initials RLD, for Robert Luis Donovan. Painfully he closed it and turned to Joe. "Where did you get it?"

Joe had a practiced answer. "Card game. Phoenix."

"Who from?"

"Some dude."

"What did he look like?"

"I don't remember. I was drunk. You want it or not?"

"I'll give you ten dollars for it."

"I need twenty."

Chance, determined to get his hands on the watch, gave in and paid him twenty dollars in gold coin. He then secured the watch in his vest pocket.

The gambler staggered away and returned to the card table where Colby and three others were waiting.

Colby looked up as Chance came by and paused at the table. "You want something, marshal?"

"Aren't you supposed to be in jail in Globe?"

"Got out two days ago."

Chance looked at Joe, who kept his head down, and he reluctantly left the saloon.

Outside, Chance mounted his buckskin and paused to look again at the watch with an aching heart.

*   *   *   *

Under a cloudy sky, Pearl came out of her cabin early the next morning. She was wearing a long duster over her pretty blue dress and her dark hair was tied back with a ribbon.

She was on her way to work but paused near the trough. She saw Joe coming across the street and had the urge to run but stood her ground as he walked over to her.

"Joe, I'm on my way to work."

He wasn't sober, but neither was he drunk. He was just a worn-out mess.

"I haven't had any sleep," he said. "Can I bunk in your cabin?"

"No."

He rubbed his eyes. "Why not?"

"Lester would fire me."

That sank in, and he moved to put his hand on the rail by the trough. There were no horses there, so he lingered.

"As I said, I have to go to work," she said and started walking north to the restaurant.

Joe was severely disappointed but having a bad headache from the night before, he decided to let it pass. He drummed up some of his charm.

"Pearl, everything will change for us, just as soon as I get my fortune."

"Yes, your grandfather in Denver," she said, not looking back.

Pearl, so lonely it hurt, was no longer interested in Joe's promises. She could not forget she was married, and if she were not, she would have ignored Joe and tried to capture the marshal.

At the moment, she only thought about earning more money to send to Canada before Fred was released from jail.

*   *   *   *

Weeks later at East Ridge, Pearl, wearing a long coat over her blue dress, saw Joe riding up to the rail by the trough. She had just left her cabin and was on the stone path leading to Lester's Restaurant. He looked dashing as ever.

He dismounted, walked over, and took both of her hands. "I won some money last night. I want to buy you something. Hey, is that a tear?"

"I just got another letter from my brother. My mother needs to be in the hospital for a long time, and he says it will cost over a thousand dollars."

"The same brother who's been borrowing money all this time? And you still believe him?"

"He's the only one in my family who ever answers my letters."

They stopped at a bench, out of earshot of the customers, and sat down.

She nodded. "And I only have a few dollars saved. Can you help? A loan?"

"Honey, I won a big hand, but I owed some people a lot of money. All I got left is twenty dollars of my own. But don't worry, we'll think of some way to get it."

"There is no way. Not in time."

"Hey, I know a trick. I'll spot some rich joker. You invite him in some night. He'll think he's having his way. I'll be hiding in the bedroom and yell I'm your husband and make him pay."

She shook her head, angered. "You really think I'd pull a stunt like that?"

"Well, okay, but they're talking about closing the mines down real soon." He grinned, waving a hand. "We could rob a bank."

She finally looked amused. "You ever do that?"

"Maybe."

"This is serious, Joe, and I have to go to work."

She stood and walked to the restaurant.

Joe, stood now, sobered, and watched after her. He turned to the street where he had left his horse at the rail near the trough.

Later that darkening day with drizzling rain, Pearl, wearing her coat, walked out of the restaurant with Lester and away from the tables, out of earshot but under the roof overhang. She had asked for a private talk.

Pearl was pleading for a loan. "I'd pay you back, something every week."

"I can't, Pearl. The mines are sure to close, and I'm deep in debt already. Don't you have any friends? I mean, except that Joe Boot?"

"I don't think a woman can count on any man, not anymore."

"Now, you can't believe that."

"If women ever get the vote, there'll be a lot of changes."

"Wow, you're one of them, huh?" Lester grinned, hoping to cheer her and soften his being unable to help. "So, what would you change?"

"If a man beats his wife or steals from her, he'll go to jail."

"That's right personal. What else?"

"Women as delegates to Washington. Judges, mayors, or bankers. Even President."

"So, who will have the babies and keep house, then?"

"We'll have the babies but men can learn how to use a broom."

They both laughed.

"I see how you look at Donovan. I bet if he crooked his little finger, you'd forget all about your crusade."

"I'm married, Lester. Besides, Mr. Donovan is made of brick. He has no feelings."

They walked back inside.

*   *   *   *

Later that fall of 1898, Chance visited Sheriff Truman in the latter's local office in Florence on a rainy afternoon. Truman had several offices but Florence was where he and his family lived, so he considered it his hometown.

Chance found Truman with his boots up on his desk, half asleep.

Coffee steamed on the iron stove, and the cells were empty. It was a simple office with racks of rifles, a few gunbelts, and some boxes of recovered property. Posters were plastered on a wall.

Truman looked up as Chance entered, dropped his boots, and stood. They shook hands.

Chance noticed Truman was agitated as he pointed to the coffee.

They walked over to the stove, helped themselves. Truman sat back at his desk and Chance pulled up a chair in front of it.

Truman grunted. "More steers being run off. They seem to just plumb disappear. Not a single mining camp admits to eating stolen beef. Sure keeps me busy."

Chance nodded and sipped his coffee as Truman continued.

"You been to East Ridge lately?"

"A few weeks back."

"I hear the mines are having serious flooding." He leaned forward. "How was Pearl Hart? You know her old man got out of jail and took off again?"

"I got no say in what she does. And I have no time for thinking about it. I have a job to do."

"Just like Texas. Big Chance Donovan. Does his job. Don't look right or left. Just keeps to himself. No time for women. Sounds pretty lonely, Chance."

"Joe Boot's been hanging around her."

"That gambler dude?"

"There's more to 'im than he lets on." Chance took out his father's gold watch. "He had this for sale. Claims he won it in a card game in Phoenix."

"Your pa's?"

"Has his initials, just the way I remember."

Chance flipped the back open, then closed it and pocketed it in his vest. He had come to accept he might never learn who had shot his adoptive father, but the Boxers were still prime suspects.

Truman stood when Chance got to his feet.

"About the Boxers," Truman said. "They were extradited to

Texas. But the Mason brothers were sent up to Canon City to serve out a life sentence for murder. They escaped the courthouse up there, some ten years ago."

"So I heard."

Truman hesitated but had to ask. "At the Beehive, I got the feeling you had more than one axe to grind with Trey Boxer. Like you had another history with him, personal like."

Chance looked grim and nodded. "But he doesn't remember, and it was a long time ago. So let's leave it at that."

"Okay, so where you headed?"

"Some ranchers on the border sent for me."

"More rustling?"

"Yes, and one of their hands was found murdered."

*   *   *   *

In February of 1899, at East Ridge mining camp, Pearl was retiring for the night and had just turned down the lamp in the other room to go to bed. She wore a wrapper over her night dress.

Her cabin was simple. There was an iron stove, still hot as she let the fire burn for awhile longer. A table and chairs. A big dresser with a mirror on it. The windows had no curtains but were shuttered for the night.

Suddenly, there was an abrupt knocking on the back door.

Pearl came out of the bedroom, took her pistol from the gunbelt resting on the table. It had been given to her by Joe for her safety. She moved closer to the back door.

Another knock. Then Joe Boot was calling in a low voice. "Pearl! It's Joe. Let me in! I've been shot!"

Pearl hesitated, then unbarred the door and stepped back to allow him inside. She replaced the bar as he hurried to a chair at the table and sat down. There was a bloody bandana wrapped around his left shirt sleeve. He had his coat around his shoulders and dropped it as he grimaced in pain.

Pearl set the pistol aside and came to untie the bandanna. She pulled his shirt far enough from his left shoulder to free his arm from the sleeve. His upper arm was bleeding. Joe could not bear to look at the blood and averted his face.

Pearl filled a bowl with water still hot in the kettle. She brought it to the table and used a towel to wash the wound. Standing at his side, she could feel him shudder at her every stroke of the towel.

"Bullet went right through," he gasped.

"Who did it?"

"Some sneak took a shot at me in the dark. Over by the saloon." He grimaced as she worked on him. He could not bring himself to watch. "I win at cards, Pearl. Any one of them sore losers could've done it."

"I didn't hear a shot."

"You were inside some pretty thick walls."

"If you're winning, maybe you could help me with a loan, to send to Canada."

"I can't do that, Pearl. I only won about ten dollars."

Pearl managed to wrap his upper arm in a clean cloth and tied it. She saw a burn on the same arm just above the wrist. "That's a bad burn. From a running iron?"

"Where'd you get that idea?"

"I don't believe your story."

"Pearl, you got to be more trusting of me."

79

She found balm to coat the burn and then wrapped it. She pulled his sleeve down over it and gave him the rest of the coffee, still warm from the pot.

"You don't have any whiskey in here?"

"Never." She sat at the table opposite him. "Lester says the mines are shutting down and he'll be closing his restaurant by the end of the week."

"Yeah, so I heard." He sipped the coffee, still grimacing with pain.

"But," she said, "Lester says he can get me a job in Globe at a friend's restaurant and even gave me a letter to take along. I just don't know if it's soon enough. My brother wrote that my mother won't live without an operation. I have to do something before Fred finds me again."

"Pearl, I been watching the Globe stage. Half the time there's no shotgun guard."

Pearl was only half listening. She cleaned blood from the outside of his sleeve and then wrapped a clean bandanna around the outside of it.

She was sad. "I wrote Marshal Donovan, hoping he'd vouch for me at the bank in Globe, so I could borrow some money, but he never answered."

Joe quickly lied. "I heard he was telling folks you wasn't decent, taking up with me while you was still married."

Upset, she wasn't sure whether it was true. "He said that?"

"That's what I heard, but you know what? Globe is rich in silver, and I could win some big pots in one of the back rooms."

"Lester said there were nice people there, and with the right clothes, I could be one of them. And even sing in the choir at the church."

"But you don't have money for clothes."

"Lester sent some to the ladies' shop and gave me a letter."

Joe felt he was losing control and didn't want to leave.

She went to the iron stove, poked at the fire, put in a stick of wood. "I can't sleep now."

He grinned. "I could help you sleep." At her glare when she turned, he gestured. "Ain't we been together long enough? Don't you trust me? Pearl, I want to marry you. Write your old man, ask him to set you free."

"My church won't allow it. And if you're around when he shows up, he might just shoot you down."

"I thought he was in jail again."

"I don't know for sure."

"Pearl, he takes every cent you save when you need it for your mother. Why do you let him rough you up?"

"He's my husband. Your law doesn't protect me."

"My law?"

"You're a man, aren't you? Have you seen any women voting lately?"

"Oh, that again." Joe stood and looked her over with lust. "How about us?" He moved closer. "I'm tired of waiting."

She lifted the long iron poker near the stove and waved it. "'Go home."

He stopped, seeing she was about to whack him and realizing he only had one good arm at the moment. "Gees, Pearl."

"There'll be no bedding down."

"Everybody already assumes…"

"Everybody? Is that what you've been telling the marshal?"

"No, but, well, maybe he heard about it."

"He hasn't been here to check on me, not for months… And

81

he never answered my letter. Is that why? Because he thinks I'm... with you?"

"I just wanted him to know where I stand."

She half swung the poker. "Get out of here!"

Joe shook his head, favored his bleeding arm, took up his coat and hat. She raised the poker as if to strike.

"But I love you, Pearl! I even shared my claim with you."

"It came up empty and you know it. All that work and blisters for nothing."

"But I'll make it up to you, honest."

She raised the poker again, and he retreated out the back door. She hurried to close and bar it. Tears in her eyes, she wondered what the marshal was thinking of her.

At the same time, she was all alone except for Joe, and he had been kind to her, if a little too romantic at times.

She knew that if Fred got out of jail again, he would appear, looking for her savings. She still had the bruises on her arms and sides where he had abused her in his search for money. She knew of no law to protect her from him because he was her husband, nor did she think women would achieve such a law in the near future.

* * * *

In the spring of 1899, Globe was a small but busy town among rolling hills in a land of green and red and gold. Wagons pulled in and out with farmers bringing their crops to sell. A stagecoach was still operating. The Arizona Eastern Railroad had been running for several years but it only had one route, and the stage went everywhere.

Javelina were hunted in the desert for sport. Pronghorns ran free. To the east of town, the San Carlos Reservation still had difficulty holding its residents. Further north, the Salt River canyon with its purple, orange, red and blue was a popular recreation area. Beyond to the east was the Fort Apache Reservation.

For nearly two weeks, Pearl had worked happily in the kitchen in Mary's Fine Restaurant. She still hoped to earn enough to send money for her mother's care in Canada. She bought a nice print dress and a pretty shawl to wear to church, where she will be singing in next Sunday's choir. She had not heard from Fred since she arrived. Joe Boot had only visited twice but had not stayed in town.

Nor had she seen the marshal. He never had answered her letter.

She had a small cabin to herself to the right of the restaurant and some distance back from the street. A stone path led to it from the boardwalk.

On that first bright Sunday when she would sing, ladies and gents arrived in their finery at the Globe Community Church. Children skipped and laughed as they followed their parents inside.

Pastor Schmidt—mid-forties, dowdy in black with a pious smile—greeted the people as they entered.

For Pearl, wearing her new Sunday dress, the pastor had a special smile, a soft handshake. He had heard her sing for the choir director—a young teacher at the local school—and both had been very impressed. Pearl was not yet aware that the pastor had a yen for her.

In the small choir of two men—one, the director—and six women, Pearl Hart wore the blue robe, looking beautiful with her dark hair on her shoulders. For the first time in that church, Pearl sang in her beautiful voice. The congregation could only listen in admiration. Men could not take their eyes from her.

As a finale and solo, she sang a favorite and beautiful, fast-paced hymn:

> *"When the trumpet of the Lord shall sound,*
> *and time shall be no more,*
> *And the morning breaks, eternal, bright and fair,*
> *When the saved of earth shall gather,*
> *over on the other shore,*
> *And the roll is called up yonder, I'll be there."*

The chorus was sung along with her by the choir.

Pastor Schmidt paid Pearl special attention at all times, while his portly, pale wife watched from a side door in her drab, pale dress.

Among the congregation was a group of eight stuffy, frowning women. Their leader, Mathilda Grey—a pretty woman in her forties with the finest attire—was the leader of the Church Women's League for Decency. Next to her sat the older Mrs. Fine, also very snooty.

Seated on the other side of Mathilda, her husband, the rugged Hiram Grey, drooled over Pearl as she sang and even during the closing of the service, while Mathilda glared at him.

Everyone filing out of the church was greeted at the exit by the pastor.

As Pearl left with some of the choir, the pastor took her hand, drew her aside, smiled and thanked her. Pearl, feeling uncomfortable, retrieved her hand. Some couples stopped Pearl to praise her singing.

Two bachelors paused to take her hand and smile in praise with slight bows.

Mathilda, just down the boardwalk with three of her stuffy friends, watched Pearl cross the street. "Shameful hussy. I've heard stories that would make you blush. She actually wore men's pants to work in a mine in the mountains. She sang in a saloon up there!"

"Should we tell the pastor?" one woman asked.

"I did, but he just seems to want her to sing all the more." Mathilda smirked. "But I'm not through with her yet."

CHAPTER EIGHT

The following Monday in late afternoon, Pearl was done for the day at the restaurant. She walked out into the sunlight and felt pretty in her print dress. She raised her parasol.

Pearl felt good. She was in a new community where few knew of her. She had status, sang in the choir. She had not heard from Joe Boot since his early visits, and so far, no sign of Fred, or the marshal.

Mary Shore, the restaurant owner, a little lady with grey hair and a winning smile, came to join her. She gestured toward Mathilda's fancy white house across the street. It had a white picket fence and bright flowers. They could see the woman in her expensive clothes standing near the porch swing with her husband. Hiram Grey took his wife's arm, led her down the steps, out to the boardwalk, and away toward the center of town. Mathilda, nose in the air, looked back over her shoulder at them.

Watching the couple walk away, Pearl turned to Mary. "Who is she?"

"That's Mathilda Grey. Head of the Women's League for Decency. She kind of runs this end of town. Her husband got rich on silver."

Mary went back inside.

Pearl walked around the restaurant and toward her little cabin where flowers lined the stone path.

She saw the pastor coming around the building to her left. He came hurriedly to stand on the path ahead of her. She lowered her parasol. He had never visited her here, and it made her nervous.

Hat in hand, he walked forward to greet her.

"Pastor?"

"Mrs. Hart, my child, the ladies have forced me to talk with you. They ask that you do not sing in the choir. Or attend church."

She was stunned, hurt. "Why?"

"It's the way you live, my child, with your husband away."

"I'm all alone here."

"They know of your unsavory relationship with this gambler, Joe Boot. He's been seen going to your cabin."

"But he's just a friend. He doesn't stay here. We had supper at Mary's, that's all."

The pastor tucked his hat under his arm and put his hands together as if praying. "You must not have this man in your home if you want to be forgiven."

"Forgiven? For what?"

"You must not have him visit."

"Let me tell you something, Pastor. I was raised in the arms of the Lord, and I know that whatever voice I have, it was a gift from Him. And He knows I have never been unfaithful to my husband."

"And where is your husband?"

"I don't know."

"There are other churches here waiting to steal my congregation. One mistake like this, and I'm out of a job. Don't you understand, Miss Pearl? I need you to stay away."

He stood uncomfortably close. She lowered her parasol between them and backed away, chin up.

"They don't want me," she said, "then I sure don't want them. Or your church."

"But you are in need of counseling, of comfort."

"Not now."

Unsure of his lascivious intentions, she whirled her parasol and walked to her front door, entering and slamming it behind her. She barred the door and peered out the curtains to see him hesitate, then turn away.

She kicked at the wall, grimaced at hurting her foot, sat down in a chair with her hands over her face as she burst into tears.

Early the next morning, Pearl opened her door to leave for work in the light of a bright sunrise.

As she turned to close it, saw a paper stuck on the outside, written in charcoal: HARLOT.

Pearl turned to see Mrs. Fine hurrying away and chased after her.

"Stop right there!" Pearl shouted.

Mrs. Fine hurried to the edge of the boardwalk and lifted her skirts as if to cross.

Pearl ran up behind her, swung her parasol, and whacked her on the rear.

Mrs. Fine squealed, jumped, didn't turn, and hurried across

the boardwalk without looking back. She headed for Mathilda's house but no one was on the porch.

Pearl returned to her front door, took down the paper, tore it to shreds, threw the pieces down and grounded them into the dirt with her heel. At the same time, tears rolled down her face.

She locked her door, wiped her face with her handkerchief, and turned, chin in the air. She lifted her parasol and walked proudly up the street to enter the front door of the restaurant.

Later that evening, Mary followed Pearl outside as a few customers left at the same time. The two women walked out of earshot and stood on the boardwalk.

They looked across the street at Mathilda's house, and saw her with Mrs. Fine and three other women on the grand porch, all perched as if they owned the town.

Mary turned to the frustrated Pearl. "We had almost no business today. Just a few bachelors. I heard from people who said they can no longer come to my restaurant. I have to let you go, Pearl. Lets go back in, and I'll give you your pay."

"But if I work in the kitchen, they won't see me."

"They didn't see you today and we had only a handful of customers." Mary took her hand and smiled kindly. "Don't you see, Pearl? Those women are jealous of you. Of your voice. Of how pretty you are. And they hate how their men look at you."

"But I need work!"

"Don't you have anyone to help you?"

"My friend Joe. He'll be by tomorrow in the morning. But he never has much money either."

"The new cook arrives tomorrow and he has a family. They need the cabin. You can stay tonight but you need to be out before noon. Meanwhile, come inside and I'll give you your pay for the last two days."

"That may at least get me a ticket on the stage. Somewhere."

The next morning at first light, Pearl got up and packed her bags. Still in her gown and wrapper, she wiped at a tear rolling down her cheek.

She fingered the locket dangling at her throat. She took the gunbelt from the hook by the door and was about to take it with its .38 pistol to her carpet bag. Joe's gift had given her comfort that someone cared enough to be sure she was safe.

There was a knock at the door.

Pearl replaced the gunbelt on the hook and stood by the door. "Who is it?"

Pastor Schmidt called from outside. "I have good news, my child."

Pearl hesitated, then opened the door. He stood, looking pious, hat in hand. "May I come in? I think we may have a solution to your church attendance."

Pearl tightened the belt on her wrapper, and let him inside, as he closed the door behind him.

She was clearly upset. "You're coming here, it don't look no better than my friend Joe."

Hat still in hand, he sat on the couch. "My dear, there is a big difference. I'm a man of God. I'm here to minister to you."

"I just lost my job and my home."

"But I can fix that, if you let me."

"Coffee?"

"Yes."

She went to the stove, unaware he was taking off his shoes

and unbuttoning his britches, then getting to his feet. As she filled a cup with coffee, she was suddenly aware that he was right behind her and breathing down her neck.

Pearl turned to find him so close, she had to stumble back near the table to get away. He was so passionate, he wasn't aware she was struggling to escape. His britches were open in front, and he was shoeless in his white sox.

"The solution," he said, "is for you to be under my protection."

Pearl was now backed up against the table.

He leaned so close, his breath was on her face. "My wife understands that I must reach out to the unworthy."

She squirmed away from him, but he followed as she backed toward the door.

He took her right hand. "Let me make you worthy, Pearl."

He tried to kiss her, but she stomped on his stocking covered left foot and he yelled.

She brought up her knee to his groin, fast and hard.

He gasped, fell back, and doubled over.

"You hypocrite!" she said, jerking open the door. "Get out!"

"Wait, my shoes!"

He frantically tried to pull up his britches, all the while, terrified he would be seen.

She shoved him. Still doubled over in pain and groaning, he staggered backward to the open door.

Pearl shoved him outside, into the sunlight. He was bouncing around in his stocking feet in the dirt, still trying to get his britches buttoned.

Pearl tossed his shoes outside.

"I will tell everyone you attacked me," he said. "I came to minister, and you reacted by hitting me!"

"That's just fine," she said. "Then I'll finish the job."

She grabbed the pistol from the holster, cocked it, and brought it outside.

"No, no, I was only making a joke."

She fired at the ground by his feet. The pastor grabbed his shoes and ran around her cabin to rush for cover behind the buildings nextdoor with his britches still unbuttoned. He soon disappeared, wimpering in agony.

Across the way, Mathilda and her husband had been standing on their porch, watching.

Pearl looked over at Mathilda and waved the pistol at her and her husband. They hurriedly went inside.

Before Pearl could catch her breath, Joe Boot, who had just arrived in town, reined up and dismounted.

He grinned at her. "I saw your visitor running for his life."

"That was the pastor, wanting to make me 'worthy'."

Joe walked over and took the pistol as her hand was shaking. "Come on, let me have some coffee and you can tell me all your troubles."

Pearl, glad to see a friendly face, walked inside with him.

Pearl, still in her wrapper, was badly shaken as she sat on her couch. Joe poured two cups of coffee and sat at her side. She was in tears as she told her story.

"No job. No money. And the whole town thinks I'm a sinful woman. With you."

"If they only knew. But I should have been here."

"I miss my children. My mother is dying. I can't borrow the money. It's been months since I wrote the marshal to see if he'd help me at the bank. He never even answered. I have no idea if

Fred will just show up some day. Why am I being punished?"

"It's them, little lady. This is no place for us. We got things to do, places to go."

"Where?"

"I been using the shack at my old claim."

She realized then that he was her only hope. "All right, but I don't have a horse."

"Finish packing. I'll reload your pistol. And then we'll go to the livery and get you one."

"But I don't have any money."

"I have enough from my last winnings."

Desperate to leave town, she went into the bedroom to dress and finish packing.

Joe did not try anything with her because he needed her to go with him. He had plans that did not include a useless mine.

Pearl went along with him. She felt she had no choice. The livery owner was impressed with the claim Joe showed him, because Joe lied and said he had just won it in a card game, so maybe it was a rich one. Just the same, Joe was unable to convince the man that he would send money to later pay for the horse and had to give him ten dollars for a tired sorrel mare and a saddle with cracked leather.

Days later, Pearl and Joe rode through the ghost town of East Ridge. When they reached his shack deep in the mountains, they settled inside as he built a fire in the hearth. She remained fully dressed because she didn't want any romantic attention.

"I have to find a job," she said. "I'm a good cook. Maybe at some other mining camp."

"Most of the mines are being flooded out. Everywhere."

She sat staring at the red and yellow flames sparking from the log in the hearth. She did not even have the funds to go home, and even if she did, she'd be too ashamed to face them after Fred's treatment and jail time. And with all the rumors haunting her life.

After they had eaten and were having their coffee at the table, Joe said his piece.

"So, there's a way we can make money, in a hurry. With the Globe stage."

"Joe, I told you I can't do that."

"There's no shotgun guard. They stop for water, and we step out, hold our guns on them, get their money, and they leave. No one gets hurt."

So desperate she felt she had to listen, she yet shook her head. "They'd recognize me."

"In boys clothes? Your hair up in your hat? Bandana over your face? You don't have to say anything. Just cover them while I relieve them of their money."

Pearl shivered, her face in her hands. She knew she was weakening.

And Joe was persuasive. "No one will get hurt, I swear. After the job, we send them on their way. A real adventure."

Pearl picked up on the word adventure. She looked up, gazed at him. A yearning for adventure had been her undoing the moment she had met Fred Hart. Except that, right now, she was hurt, humiliated, and desperate for money.

"You and me, Pearl. And a lot of money. For your ma. And then we'll go to California."

Pearl got up, walked over to the stove, refilled her coffee cup.

Joe continued. "Nobody cares but me, don't you see that?"

She sat back down and nodded, because she felt it was true.

Joe gestured. "We slip out tonight. Catch the stage in the morning, right near that water hole near the springs, where they stop to rest the horses. You won't have to say or do anything, just be there to hold a pistol on 'em so I won't get shot."

Pearl, gloomy, stared into her cup.

He suddenly grinned, wanting to cheer her. "You sure sent that preacher packing. I don't think he's going to be very popular with the ladies."

She had to smile. "Or his wife."

CHAPTER NINE

It was cold and windy that late afternoon on May 29, 1899. Kane's Springs Canyon, between Globe and Riverside, was a few miles north of the Gila River. The stage road followed a creek lined with tall green cottonwoods and stunted junipers, down through a long red and yellow canyon, headed for the break at the water hole and springs.

In the nearby bushes amid sweet-smelling yellow flowers and dark pines, on foot and with their horses out of sight, Boot and Pearl got ready. He was almost as nervous as she was, but there was no turning back.

Pearl wore a loose, oversized boy's green flannel shirt that hid her figure, along with boys' baggy tan trousers and her boots. Her hair was tucked up under a white sombrero with a wide floppy brim and chin strap. A red bandanna covered her face, up to just over her nose, held partly in place by the chin strap.

Joe wore uncharacteristicly sloppy tan miners' clothes, a brown poncho, a red polka dot bandana over his face, and a Mexican sombrero with flowered band on his head. He carried a gunny sack and his Colt .45, which he held in his right hand.

Pearl held the .38 Joe had once given her—the same one she'd used to fire at the terrified pastor—in both trembling hands. She was numb and frightened.

Pearl had calmed her horse but her own emotions were in turmoil. 'It's for my mother,' she thought. 'And because of all those people who were mean to me. And because I have no where else to turn. So please, forgive me, dear Lord.'

Joe adjusted his bandana as he continued to use his wiles.

He whispered, "You don't have to speak. Just try to look dangerous."

Pearl's furtive glance betrayed her fear.

Joe tried to reassure her, "It'll be over real fast. No one will get hurt. Be brave. Remember your nasty husband. And that lecherous old preacher. Those snobbish old ladies. Nasty notes on your front door. Money you need for your mother's care. And then, how my share will take us to California for a brand new adventure where no one knows who we are."

Pearl hesitated, bit her lip, then balanced her pistol.

They could hear the stage coming and soon it was there. It was pulled by four bay horses held in check by the aging driver, Henry Bacon. His drooping mustache seemed to echo how tired he was.

Inside the stage were three male passengers. It came into the clearing near the water hole, and bumped and swayed as Bacon pulled it to a halt.

He didn't see Pearl and Joe hidden in the trees.

As the driver relaxed his lines, Joe came out of hiding, followed by Pearl, who stayed back but could be seen with a wavering pistol.

Joe aimed his revolver at the driver and simulated a Mexican accent.

"Halt!"

The driver raised his hands in disbelief.

"Toss your pistol," Joe ordered, and when the driver obeyed, Joe, seeing it was a new model with a pearl handle, picked it up and tossed it to Pearl, who let it lay at her feet. "And your long gun."

"Don't carry one," the driver said. "Nobody's ever stopped us before."

Joe Boot ordered the three passengers out with their hands up and to toss down their pistols, carried by the two white men. The third passenger, a Chinaman, was unarmed.

Pearl stayed back near the trees, pistol in both hands. She was shaking from head to foot, a nervous bundle of fear.

Joe, standing near the coach, kept his pistol handy and continued to have the driver keep his hands in the air.

In due time, Joe had relieved all of the passengers of their possessions, including a silver watch, all of which he dropped into a gunny sack.

He checked inside the coach to be sure there were no stashed weapons or purses inside. Joe then gallantly handed each a dollar in return. "For room and board. Señors."

The passengers were forced to stand and wait outside the coach.

Joe gestured to the driver. "Throw down your strong box."

"Don't have one. Just the mail," the driver said.

"Toss it down, señor."

The driver reached under the seat, took out the mailbag and tossed it down.

The passengers watched, fearful.

Pearl kept her weapon on everyone as Joe went to the canvas bag and knelt.

Joe opened it and found just a few letters, with only one fat enough to hold currency, which it did, but only twenty dollars, which he took.

Pearl looked anxiously at Joe. He shook his head. No letters for her.

Joe gestured to the driver. "Now get going. All of you."

The passengers scrambled to get back inside.

The driver hesitated. "Can't leave without the mail. Or watering the horses."

Joe put the mail back in the bag. He tossed it up to the driver, who caught it.

"We'll be watching from the trees until you leave," Joe said, forgetting his accent. "The passengers have to stay inside. Any mischief and you're all dead."

Joe backed over to Pearl, held up the sack for her to drop in the driver's pearl-handled pistol. At that moment, a lock of her dark hair dangled down her left ear.

The driver saw but turned away, pretending he had not.

"Don't follow us," Joe told them. "You will not be welcome in Mexico."

Joe and Pearl backed into the trees with the horses and waited until the coach left.

"Let's water our own horses," he said. "And fill our canteens."

Pearl was shaking so bad, she had trouble breathing. She pushed the lock of hair back under her hat.

Joe squeezed her left arm. "Told you we wouldn't have to shoot."

She holstered her pistol. "I took the shells out before we came."

Joe stared at her and laughed. They took the horses to the water hole. She filled the canteens at the nearby spring. He counted the money and grinned as she returned.

"Over four hundred, Pearl, and a solid silver watch."

"It's not very much," she said, disappointed.

"We'll split it when we get out of here, but right now, we'd better high-tail it."

*   *   *   *

In Florence early the next morning under a clear blue sky, Truman had ordered a deputy to form a posse. Meanwhile, he prepared himself in his office.

Truman was packing his saddle bag when Chance entered.

"Glad you're here, Chance."

"I got the word in Phoenix. That stage carried the U.S. Mail, and some of it was stolen, so I'm riding with you."

"Sure enough. And once we get out of my jurisdiction, we'll need your badge. Right now, we figure they could be anywhere. Sheriff Armstrong, over in Globe, is getting his own posse together, but he's heading south. He figures they're headed for the border. And we're heading north. No telling which way is right."

"Any identifications?"

"Faces were covered, but the driver said one of 'em was a woman with black hair she had stuffed under her hat. She was dressed like a man. The fellah was tall in rough clothes with a sombrero, tried to talk like a Mexican."

"And?" Chance felt pain in his chest.

Truman shook his head sadly. "Armstrong figures it was Joe Boot and Pearl Hart. Both are gone from Globe. If they got the passenger's silver watch and the driver's fancy pistol on 'em, or any of the mail, we'll have to arrest 'em."

Chance recoiled, looked away. His face darkened with his own sad thoughts.

"Poor girl," Truman said. "Every man she's known has let her down."

"Seems like."

Truman readied to go. "I got a hunch they may be hiding up at East Ridge, now that it's a ghost town."

"Maybe. I checked the claim filings. Boot has one himself not far from there, but it may be hard to find."

"We'll get old Tom."

Days later, Pearl and Joe Boot arrived at his isolated claim. It was deep in rocky terrain, but the one room log-and-adobe cabin was in the open. Pearl stayed in her boys clothes for the time being and slept on one of the two cots.

Joe had kept his distance because he wanted her to calm down and also to stay with him. He had plans for her, but was in no rush. He wanted her safely in his debt first.

The next morning, at her insistence, they walked back into the mine. It was deep and damp. He set out a lantern.

"I still think there's something in it," she said.

After a few hours of digging and chipping away at the mine walls, Joe cried out.

"Look, Pearl, silver!"

Weary, she hurried over and peered at it in the lamplight.

"That's not silver."

"Yeah, it is. Copper's wrapped around it."

But after another day of digging, Joe had to admit it was a false alarm.

He had been good to her all this while, not trying to have her in his arms. One morning, he got off his bunk as she was making coffee. Both were still in work clothes.

"Well, it's time to head for California. Are you going to stay in those britches?"

"No, I want to feel like a woman again." She sipped her coffee."But you said we'd split the money and I could mail some to my mother."

"It's still in the sack, Pearl. We'll stop somewhere on the way. We can't take a chance on anyone knowing about this claim."

"Let's split the money now."

"Don't you trust me?"

"Joe, I helped you commit robbery. It's my right to take half."

"Okay, tell you what. You get dressed and I'll saddle up. Then we'll split it before we get going."

She agreed, and he went out to saddle the horses.

Joe was losing patience. She had ignored his advances. He had played along because it was his need to keep Donovan jealous. Now they were far from civilization, just the two of them. He figured he had a right, and she was in no position to fight him off.

When he went back inside the cabin unannounced, she was in her petticoats, bodice, and boots. Her white blouse, blue jacket, and navy blue split riding skirts were laid out on her bunk. She was washing her face with her hair tied back.

He came up behind her, wrapped his arms around her waist,

and started kissing her neck and shoulder. She squealed, broke free, spun away from him, and picked up her pistol.

She drew back the hammer as he backed away, startled.

"Pearl, put that down!"

"You know I'm still married!"

"But Pearl, honey, we're in this together."

"Get out of here."

He backed away, out the open door into the sunlight.

She followed, waving her pistol.

"Don't you ever put your hands on me again!"

Her eyes wide, she gasped as she looked past him at the posse. There was Sheriff Truman, old Tom, and Deputy U.S. Marshal Chance Donovan.

Shamed, tearful, she lowered her pistol.

Joe turned to see why she was shaken. Facing the posse, he folded.

Though it was very painful for Pearl, it was all the more shattering for Chance.

Truman did all the talking while Chance kept his distance.

Pearl was allowed to dress after Tom searched the cabin and removed any weapons.

Truman took charge of the gunny sack with the stolen cash, pearl-handled pistol, and other items. Pearl, donning her hat with the chin strap, could not look at Chance or Truman. She kept her gaze down with tears in her eyes.

Nights on the road, both prisoners were tied by the ankle to a tree for sleeping. She stayed close to Joe Boot and avoided any contact with the marshal. She told herself that even if she was ever free, there would never be a day the lawman would want her now.

Chance was glad to let Truman herd the prisoners. He had no direct contact with Joe Boot, but Joe secretly wanted Chance dead.

Because Bacon, the driver, lived in Globe, the posse took the prisoners there for possible identification, but that was only an exercise. They had already found the mail bag and possessions taken from the passengers.

Riding into Globe for all to see, Pearl was ashamed. Even though she was nicely dressed as she rode with the posse, she avoided the gaze of everyone on the street. There was no one on Mathilda's porch, for which Pearl was grateful.

At the sheriff's office in downtown Globe, they learned Armstrong was still south with his posse, and that the driver, Bacon, was on a run. They were told Bacon would be laying up in Florence, where he would be available. They also learned the passengers were long gone but had left written statements.

Outside and away from the prisoners, Chance turned to Truman. "You caught 'em with the money, the pistols, and the watch. There's no choice."

"I know, but I still feel sorry for Pearl."

"We can speak for her at the trial."

"Don't give up on her yet," Truman said.

Chance shrugged because as much as he wanted to forget her, he could not.

With a crowd watching near the sheriff's office, Truman and Chance rode with the prisoners between them. Only Joe had his hands bound. Tom was no longer with them.

They were all mounted and leaving Globe the way they

had come in, by Mary's Restaurant and across from Mathilda Grey's house.

Suddenly, the Greys' front door swung open as the pastor—wild-eyed, half-dressed in pants and an open shirt, and barefoot—came charging out and stumbled down the steps to the boardwalk, then into the street.

Stepping on the little rocks in the street, he hopped about, looking terrified.

Out the front door came a furious Hiram Grey, fully dressed, six-gun in hand, dragging a half-dressed Mathilda by the hair, onto the porch. She was in white bodice and petticoats.

Hiram dropped her on the porch and fired at the pastor's feet as he leaped to the far sidewalk.

The pastor danced around, saw Sheriff Truman but didn't see Pearl, who was out of sight behind Chance. Truman rode over near him and reined up.

"Sheriff, help me!" cried the pastor.

Seeing Hiram coming down the steps, he tried to hide behind Truman.

Hiram was not deterred. Coming down his front steps, he fired into the air. The horses danced around. He did not notice Pearl or Chance as he rushed into the street.

Mathilda rose up on her porch, saw the gathering crowd staring at her. She staggered to her feet, rushed back inside, and closed the door.

The pastor hovered behind the sheriff's horse and clung to the saddle strings.

Hiram walked over to the sheriff and could see the pastor's bare feet.

"Sheriff, I got a right to kill him."

"You do, you'll hang."

"Not if we were back in Texas."

Truman tried not to grin at the pastor hiding behind him.

Hiram spoke loud enough for all to hear. The crowd was beginning to laugh.

"I come back from Phoenix, and there he is, in my bed, with my wife! The worm!"

The pastor left the posse, hopped across the street toward a group of women and charged among them, seeking cover. The women scattered. The pastor scurried around, darted here and there. A woman hit at the pastor with her parasol.

The pastor ran onto the boardwalk opposite the Greys' house and ran towards the center of town.

Hiram shouted after him. "Get out of town or I'll blow off your privates!"

"Let him go," Truman said. "He's not worth it."

"He'd better not show his face in this town again." Hiram wiped his brow, holstered his pistol, talking loud enough for all to hear. "I shoulda known better'n to marry a floozy right out of a saloon."

Pearl caught her breath. Mathilda, the snob, had been a painted woman! Pearl shook her head but felt redeemed. The woman leading her departure from Globe had been a soiled dove.

Pearl felt the pastor's exposure had been redemption for herself, but she was beginning to feel sorry for him.

She was glad, however, when they rode out of town, away from the crowd.

CHAPTER TEN

B ecause newspaper reporters had surrounded the Florence jail to interview Pearl and it was becoming a spectacle, the Federal Court Judge transferred her out of town to the Pima County Jail in Tucson, where her presence was a secret for some time, and public access was limited to street observation. It was October of 1899.

The middle-aged guard was kind to Pearl and brought her extra food and coffee.

"I heard you sing in Phoenix," he had said.

"The judge is just being mean, sending me here," had been her reply.

"But you're safer here."

She thanked him for his concern.

Her cell had adobe walls so it remained cool inside, but there was only a narrow window, set high on the wall with no bars but too small for even Pearl to slide through.

The night of October 12, 1899, the guard brought her sweet,

frosted treats and coffee. He slid the tray under the bars, and she smiled her thanks.

"Folks are on your side," he told her. "They blame Joe Boot."

"Thanks for telling me."

"My wife, on the other hand…"

He didn't finish and she nodded, because she understood.

As the guard disappeared beyond the door to the front office, closing it behind him, there was a tapping at the high unbarred window.

Excited, she stood on her bunk to see out, and there was Colby, the hard case who been at East Ridge. He was standing on an empty wooden crate in the alley outside. He handed her a knife. She had seen him with Joe, but she didn't know him personally. She wasn't sure she could trust him, but in her current circumstances, she felt she had no choice. She took the knife but did not understand.

She thought he wanted her to use it on the guard, her friend, which she would never do. She began to remember more about Colby from East Ridge. She was a little afraid of him, but she was also desperate, so she listened.

He poked another knife at the adobe frame of the window.

"You work from the inside," he whispered. "We'll cut this wall away from the bottom of the window so you can climb out."

Colby had a bigger knife as he cut away the adobe from the outside, but she helped, and soon the opening was much lower and wide enough for her to climb out with his help.

She grabbed hold of the window's lower rim and side. Colby took hold of her wrists and pulled her upward and through the window.

Before she knew it, she was falling down into his arms. He

lowered her from the crate to the ground. He had two saddled bays waiting with bedrolls, possible sacks, and saddle bags.

She didn't question why he was helping her, fearing the reason, but right then, she would do anything to escape. After that, she told herself, she would find a way to be free.

They rode quietly along a dark, back street and were soon out of town.

By morning, they were well along the trail to Deming. They stayed in the trees and brush, and off the main road.

Pearl rode astride in her dress, next to Colby, who kept watching her.

After a time, they reined up on the road. Colby turned and looked back. "Clean getaway."

"Did Joe send you?"

"No."

Pearl was grateful but leery. "Why are you helping me?"

"Why do you think?"

"You've wasted your time," she said. "I'm still married."

He ignored her and pointed ahead. "That old stage road will take us to Deming. I got friends there. We'll hop the train. No one will ever find us."

Pearl didn't answer. They kept riding until nightfall and made camp. They left the horses saddled close by but had loosened the cinches.

They didn't chance a fire and ate cold food. He took down the bedrolls and spread them side by side.

"I got a yen for you up in East Ridge," he told her. "When you was singing."

"Maybe I can find a way to pay you for helping me."

He closed in on her and grabbed her wrist, startling the horses.

"I got money. What I ain't got is you."

She fought back, struggled as he wrapped his big arms around her. He kissed her hungrily. She stomped on his foot. He yelped but kept tearing at her clothes.

She fought her way free, brought up her knee, and hit him in the groin. Hard.

Colby gasped in agony as he fell and doubled up. He managed to get up on one knee. She kicked him in the rear and he fell forward, groaning.

Pearl grabbed a food sack and a blanket. She tightened the cinch on her horse and mounted. She grabbed the reins on his mount and led it along with her, leaving him on foot.

Colby was curled on the ground, moaning in agony.

Days later, Pearl, no longer leading Colby's horse, having turned it free, came down out of the trees to the trail, and reined up by a sign with an arrow pointing ahead:

NEW MEXICO TERRITORY – 5 MILES

She kept riding. Soon she turned a corner on the road, into the open.

She found herself facing three men on horseback with badges.

"Don't worry, ma'am, we have your cohort, Mr. Colby. He'll be charged with helping a federal prisoner escape. After he gets some much needed medical attention."

The three lawman could not help but grin.

Pearl could only blush.

*   *   *   *

It was on November 15, 1899, that the trial was held in United States District Court in the Federal Court House in Florence.

A crowd had gathered around the front of the building, trying to see inside.

Reporters pushed their way forward, flashing their press cards.

In Judge Doan's courtroom, there was no nonsense allowed. His hard features and regal attitude intimidated many gathered there. Reporters were silenced at every turn. The bailiff, a big man with wide shoulders and a dangerous glint in his eyes, kept a gathering crowd out of the already packed room.

It was the second trial of Pearl for the stage robbery offense. Joe Boot had already been sentenced in the first trial. She had been found not guilty, but now faced another charge, that of stealing the driver's pistol.

Attorney Griffen, for the defense, stood beside Pearl. He was a long-time lawyer with a fine reputation. He wore a dark suit and blue striped tie, and sported a curled, black mustache.

District Attorney Stone stood near them. Clean-shaven with heavy brows, he was also wearing a dark suit, but with a plain blue tie.

The harried male clerk was writing everything down. The new jury looked tired.

Griffen made his case. "Your Honor, Mrs. Hart was acquitted of robbing the Globe stage. Mr. Boot accepted full responsibility and told the court he forced her into it." He didn't mention that Joe expected his grand gesture to get him a light sentence, not the thirty years he received. More than likely, Joe was furious.

Griffen took a deep breath. "Now, we have a new jury and she is charged with stealing a pistol from the driver, Mr. Bacon. The same occurrence. The same transaction at the very same time. And a lesser included crime. There is no justification for another trial."

Judge Doan looked at him with stern disinterest. "Your client swayed the first jury with her feminine wiles. I don't believe Mr. Boot was entirely to blame for the crime."

"Your Honor, I ask that you recuse yourself for prejudice against Mrs. Hart."

"Denied."

Griffen drew another deep breath and continued. "I have filed affidavits from U.S. Deputy Marshal Donovan and Sheriff Truman, both attesting to her decency and how she had been only a victim of circumstances beyond her control."

"So noted."

"And Your Honor," Griffen continued, "I have filed pleadings for Double Jeopardy."

Judge Doan remained impassive. "Denied."

Griffen continued. "Then I protest this formation of a second jury."

Judge Doan was ever grim. "Overruled."

In the back of the crowded courtroom, Chance stood unnoticed, hat in hand. Both he and Truman had signed support for Pearl. Even the driver had said she was more of an observer.

Chance was hurting for her and angered that her husband was nowhere to be found, likely afraid of being charged as an accomplice after the fact.

The jury returned with a rather quick decision.

Judge Doan, looking like doomsday on his bench, waited for their verdict.

Pearl and Attorney Griffen stood.

The balding jury foreman read the verdict. "We find the defendant guilty as charged."

Pearl slumped. Her attorney held her arm, keeping her upright.

Pearl was afraid to look at the jury.

Griffen continued to protest. "Your honor, I move for a new trial."

Doan remained stern. "Motion denied. Court adjourned until two o'clock for sentencing."

The clerk stood. "All rise."

Everyone stood as the judge left the courtroom by a back door to his chambers.

Now the courtroom emptied, except for the bailiff in the back by the door, and Pearl and her lawyer.

Exhausted, Pearl sat down, and her attorney sat with her.

She was confused. "Why is the judge so mad at me?"

"First off, you escaped jail at Tucson. They had to track you all the way to Deming, New Mexico Territory. As soon as you were caught, there was a crowd. You spent a lot of time signing autographs."

"What happened to Mr. Colby?"

"Not much. He was fined for damaging a public building, given ten days, and let go."

"What?"

"He told them he was in love with you, and that you offered him your favors if he helped you."

"That's a lie!"

"Justice can make mistakes, as you know." Her attorney

paused to shuffle papers, shrugged, then continued. "In the first trial, the jury fell in love with you. You were acquitted. The judge was angry. This time, he made sure."

"Joe got thirty years. What will he do to me?"

"Let's wait and see. I made clear that the pistol was only worth ten dollars. That's petty theft."

They stood as reporters crashed into the courtroom.

The bailiff intervened and marched her out a side door for holding.

Later the same day, court reconvened. The judge sat on his bench.

The crowd was hushed as Pearl and her attorney stood.

In the back of the room, Chance stood among others. He looked like he carried a heavy burden as he watched.

The judge addressed Pearl. "Mrs. Hart, you have been found guilty of robbery. Your partner has been sentenced to thirty years. Have you anything to say before I pass sentence?"

Her lawyer spoke. "My client begs for the mercy of the court."

The judge persisted. "Mrs. Hart?"

"It was for my mother. She's very ill in a hospital in Canada. My brother wrote me how they needed money."

Judge Doan was doubtful. "Where is this letter?"

"I don't have it now. I mailed it to a friend for help."

The judge frowned. "Then no evidence exists of your claim."

Griffen intervened. "Your honor, it was reasonable for Mrs. Hart to believe—"

"Are you going to quote me about the reasonable man? We have a woman here. And they are never reasonable. It's their nature." Doan was firm. "And motive holds little weight against what she did."

Pearl's anger rose out of control. "But the laws are made by men! They should not apply to women. Not until we have the vote."

The judge, already plagued by his own daughter wanting the vote, was not moved. "Mrs. Hart, be careful I do not hold you in contempt." Seeing her tears, he eased up. "I don't make the laws. I just apply them."

The judge felt sympathy for less than a minute.

"You have been found guilty of robbery," Doan said to her. "To cure you of such impulses in the future, I sentence you to five years in the Arizona Territorial Prison at Yuma. You are remanded to the sheriff." He pounded his gavel. "Court is adjourned."

Pearl nearly collapsed as her attorney caught her arm and whispered. "We'll file an appeal. And I'll write to the governor."

The clerk stood. "All rise."

The crowd stood. The judge exited to his chambers. Reporters crowded forward and tried to talk to Pearl. The bailiff ordered her away and out the side door.

Griffen turned and looked at the district attorney, who shrugged acknowledgment of some injustice.

In the back, Chance looked like he had been hit hard.

Later that same day, Chance went to Truman's office. The sheriff had already heard from a reporter, after which he had chased the newsman out of his office.

Chance walked inside. In the back, the cells held only one prisoner, asleep on his bunk.

As Chance sat facing the desk, Truman leaned forward to shove a battered, overly-inked, stamped envelope forward. "Just came for you. That letter was wrongly addressed back in May of this year. It went all the way to Florence, Alabama, and I can only guess it sat there in the dead letter office for months before someone figured out the AL was scribbled and really stood for Arizona Territory. They just sent it down from Phoenix."

Chance stared at it. The return address was Pearl's in East Ridge. It was addressed to Chance c/o Sheriff Truman. Dismayed, he sat down and slowly opened it. Enclosed was a letter from her brother in Canada.

He stared at her words and read them aloud for Truman's benefit—

> *Marshal Donovan:*
>
> *It grieves me to have to ask anyone for help but I have failed everywhere else. My mother is very ill and has been moved to a hospital in Canada. I think the bank would loan me the money to help her if you would tell them I can be trusted.*
>
> *You have been very kind to me.*
>
> *If you cannot help me, I will understand. However, I am in dire straits and have nowhere else to turn.*
>
>

Respectfully,
Pearl Hart
>

Severely stressed, Chance folded the letter, stood up, adjusted his hat, and headed out the door in a hurry.

CHAPTER ELEVEN

A short time later at the courthouse in Judge Doan's chambers, the judge was seated at his desk as he read the letters.

He handed them back to Chance, who sat facing him. "Her motive doesn't matter now. But her attorney's office is just across the street if you want to see him about this. That's all, marshal."

Chance stood up and folded the letters.

Doan leaned back. "Do you have a personal interest in this woman?"

"No, sir."

"Justice is done, marshal. Good day."

They looked sternly at each other.

Chance pocketed the letter and left.

When the judge was alone, a clerk came in to see the him. "Your Honor, your daughter is here, with another petition."

Doan looked exasperated. "Mr. Tolliver, if they ever get the vote, I'm going to retire."

"Yes, sir."

"Send her in."

The clerk left and hid his grin until he was safely in another room.

The next day, Pearl was escorted from the jail by Sheriff Truman and two deputies as they took her to the train station.

A half-dozen male reporters followed.

One reporter asked her, "Do you have plans to see Joe Boot in prison?"

Truman waved them away. "Can't you see the lady is exhausted? We have to make the train."

Pearl turned, smiled that fetching smile. "I don't know," she said. "I have no say about anything."

The reporters followed her and the sheriff all the way to the train.

In early January of 1900, Chance rode west in driving wind and sand, across the prairie, and reined up at a road sign.

YUMA TERRITORIAL PRISON — 20 MILES

Chance forced himself to ride onward.

At Yuma Prison, Pearl was isolated from the men. She wore a blue print dress of her own. Her stone cell was larger than most but still plain, dusty, and hot. It was also set aside and away from the other incarcerations.

Pearl stood and smiled as a grinning Proctor, the guard, approached the bars between them. He was middle-aged, chunky, and wearing a grey uniform with brass buttons. He was enamored with her, but not romantically. He liked her, saw her as the daughter he never had. He would do anything for her that was within his power. Extra treats often made it to her cell.

He held a stack of letters which he slid through the bars into her hands. "You sure are popular."

"But I've had no letters from my family, not before or after the trial. They must be ashamed of me. My brother hasn't written since I was sentenced. I guess he thinks I'm of no use."

"Families sometimes don't know what to write," he offered, knowing that was unlikely. "And Canada is a long way from here."

She dabbed at her eyes. "I haven't seen Joe Boot since I arrived. Have you seen him?"

"Yes, ma'am. He's been made a Trustee. He cooks for the Superintendent's family. Outside the walls."

Startled, she had to laugh. She had no idea Joe could even make coffee.

Proctor adjusted his cap. "I heard your lace handkerchiefs have already been sold. The needlepoint is nearly gone. So are your autographs."

"That's nice. I get a share and I'm saving every penny. I'll need it when my time is up. I want a new life." She hesitated. "Am I hoping for something I can't have?"

"No, Miss Pearl, you'll find a whole new world out there when you get out." He put his hand on the bar. "And your poems are real big with reporters. The Super's so impressed with your efforts, he's finally agreed to let you be an assistant to the prison baker."

"But not for him, personally."

"No, ma'am. He figures you might be a danger to Joe Boot."

That made her laugh. He reached into his pocket, took out chocolates and shared them with her.

Proctor added, "The male prisoners are sure unhappy. They miss your being there for meals. But the Super says you're a distraction and even caused some fist fights."

Pearl, flattered, smiled. Then she looked through the letters. Opened a few. "Did you ask the chaplain about my singing in the choir?"

"Yes, he's going to talk to the Super." Proctor hesitated. "And by the way, you have a visitor."

"Another reporter?"

"No, ma'am. Marshal Donovan. He's waiting in the visiting room."

Pearl brightened, then sobered. To have Chance see her in this prison was not good.

"Do I look all right?"

"Sure do." He grinned as he unlocked her cell.

In a short while, Proctor escorted her into the Visitor's Room. One other couple, a prisoner and his wife, was at a far table. Guards were watching from the back wall.

The barren room had benches along the walls and a series of tables and chairs in the center. The windows were high up and with bars.

She saw Chance, hat in hand, pacing. Her heart ached. Her face felt hot.

When he turned, the lawman stopped. He wore a new badge, U.S. Marshal, as he was no longer a deputy. He walked to a bench and waited until she sat down. He then sat near her at a respectable distance of a few feet.

She was glad to see him and smiled. "That's a new badge."

He tried to hide his distress at how pale and worn she looked.

Proctor stood near the exit door, waiting, arms folded.

Chance was tense. "I have to tell you, I got your May letter after you were sentenced. It had been all the way to Florence, Alabama, and ended up in their dead letter files, until a few months later when someone realized it went to the wrong state. I took it to the judge, along with your brother's. Didn't do any good. But I gave them to your attorney right after that."

Pearl caught her breath in relief. "So, you didn't know I was in trouble?"

"No, I'm sorry."

"I thought you were just ignoring what I wrote. But thank you for trying. I guess you know, my attorney lost on appeal. He's going to the governor next."

Chance reached into his vest, took out a letter, and offered it to her. "This came for you in Phoenix at the Liberty Hotel. From the Army. He must have given that address when he enlisted. The hotel sent it to Truman."

Pearl opened it and found a ten dollar draft from the United States Army. 'Ten dollar pay due Drummer Frederick Hart on discharge.' It was dated August of 1898.

Chance took time to shape his hat to calm himself down.

"He's been out over a year?" She stared at the check.

"Your lawyer might help you track him down."

"It's a little late for that."

"It's never too late." Chance caught himself. "I mean, to start over. You have the whole territory on your side. The newspapers, even dime novels."

She nodded, smiled, then shook her head in sudden sadness. "My daughter and son are still in Canada but now they are with my uncle. My lawyer received a letter saying he changed their last names to Brown, so no one in school would shame them. And how they never want to see me again."

"Don't believe him."

"Thank you," she whispered.

Chance didn't know what else to say or how to comfort her.

"I have to go. Just have time to get back to Florence for another trial." He stood, hat in hand, and signaled to Proctor.

She also stood. "Will you come back?"

"Yes, if I'm ever out this way."

She didn't know that he wanted to take her in his arms, to console her. She only knew how much she wanted him to do just that. They simply gazed at each other with a smile.

Proctor let him out the door, and Pearl dabbed at the tears in her eyes.

Chance was gone from her life, again.

As they left to return to her cell, Proctor grinned at her. "Everyone's in love with you. Even the marshal."

"Not him. He's all duty and law." She paused to smile. "Are you? In love with me?"

Proctor grinned. "Sure am."

She touched his arm in thanks.

*　*　*　*

In spring of the following year, 1901, not having heard from the marshal since his one visit, Pearl was lonely and miserable.

Guard Proctor came to her cell. She was sitting, doing needlepoint, but put it aside and stood as he handed more letters and magazines through the bars.

Proctor was grinning. "Bunch of women's groups are putting

pressure on the governor for parole. Heard about you singing hymns to the other prisoners and preaching from the Gospel."

"I'm grateful someone cares." Pearl looked through her mail. "Nothing from my family. And I guess there's still no word from the marshal?"

He shook his head. "But there's a dime novel in the bunch."

"They're a lot of fun. Did you know I was a sharpshooter? That I had four lovers? Nine children from different fathers? And I have hideouts in Mexico?"

"No, but you got a visitor. A pastor from Globe."

She fumed. "That hypocrite?"

"Pastor Reed?"

"Oh. I don't know him."

She hesitated, then nodded.

In the visitor's room, Pastor Reed, wearing dark grey with a white collar, was average height with a kindly face. He looked up as Pearl, looking neat and ladylike, entered the room. He held a Bible in hand and was standing.

Pearl was uncomfortable at sight of him, not knowing why he was there.

He spoke in a gentle voice. "I came all the way from Globe to apologize for Pastor Schmidt, whoever he was. We searched everywhere, but we found no record of his ever having been ordained."

"I should have known."

"There are many in the West who feel bound to serve the Lord, and they serve Him well without having the papers. But this man was a disgrace. He has since disappeared. His wife got free of him and remarried."

"Thank you for telling me," she said, feeling redeemed. "What about Hiram Grey and his wife?"

He had to smile. "Well, after Grey found her with Schmidt and chased the man off, it was in the newspaper the next day. I'm sorry I don't have a copy, but I will tell you that Mr. Grey told all. He had picked up his wife in a bawdy house run by a saloon in Denver. He arranged an annulment based on fraud, and she's said to be back in business in California."

"She was so cruel to me and had the whole town against me."

"Self-protection, I imagine, putting all the attention on you." He paused as they sat down on a bench, then spoke gently. "Are you very unhappy?"

"I don't know where my husband is, and I'll never be free, so yes, for that I am miserable. And I'm lonely here. But they have a big library. I can wear my own clothes and I sew my own dresses. I make lace kerchiefs to sell. I write poetry. Sing with the choir. And I'm free to cook in the kitchen."

He took her hand. "I have written the governor on your behalf. So have others in Globe. Mary Shore, the lady you worked for, she even led a delegation to see him."

Slightly surprised, she dabbed at a tear. "Thank her and everyone else for me."

"I was asked by Sheriff Truman to let you know what happened to that man Colby, the one who helped you escape jail in Tucson. He was shot down in Nogales when he went after another man's wife. He's buried there."

Pearl was grateful for the news. "You must think I'm a terrible person."

"No, my child. I promise you, the Lord is with you."

A few days later, the visitors room was being used for choir practice. Lemonade and cookies sat on a back table.

The chaplain, a robust figure of a man, lined them up. Pearl was the only woman among a half-dozen men who looked more like good citizens than convicts.

In the front row of the choir, Joe Boot and Pearl stood side by side.

Pearl wore a nice print dress with high collar. She looked at ease, a new woman who had found her faith once more. Joe could not take his gaze off of her.

He had hoped his gallantry at the trial would have led to a light sentence. Instead, he had been given thirty years, and he would now use it to make her feel guilty and maybe more vulnerable.

Yes, he still had plans to use her to torment Donovan until his uncle and cousins could be out, one way or another, to finish the kill. He had already sent a lot of money to get unsavory help in getting them free.

Joe whispered to Pearl, "Little lady, you look gorgeous."

"Thank you," she murmured. "Some women from the church in Globe, they sent me material for this new dress."

A piano had been wheeled inside and "Amazing Grace" was being played. Pearl sang a verse in her lovely voice. With other hymns, Joe Boot sang in a surprisingly grand voice.

A guard came to the door, signaled the chaplain, who left while the guard stayed. The choir group retreated to the back table to sit down for cookies and lemonade.

Joe and Pearl moved away from the others, out of earshot, and both smiled.

She was impressed. "I didn't know you could sing."

"There's no end to my talents." He paused. "You going back to Hart if he shows up?"

"I hope he stays away. I need a new start."

"You could have that with me."

"Joe, I never got a chance to thank you for trying to help me with the judge."

"I had to try."

"But now you'll be here a very long time."

"Don't be so sure," he whispered. "I'd take you with me, but you'd die out there in the desert."

Her voice was hushed. "Joe, don't try it. No one ever makes it."

"My uncle's locked up in Huntsville, but I sent men to help him escape if he can. And now he's sending someone to help me. A guy just released. When I'm safe, I'll send for you."

"No, I'm sorry, Joe. I'm staying. When I do leave here, I need a new life where I'm blessed, not scorned."

They paused as the chaplain returned.

*　　*　　*　　*

Two weeks later, outside the prison walls, Joe Boot left the superintendent's two story house where he worked as a cook. There was no moon yet.

He removed his apron. He was in the open.

The guard who was to take him back inside the prison sat in front of a post, sound asleep.

Joe Boot carefully moved around him.

He gazed longingly at the rifle across the guard's lap, then thought better of it.

Joe turned, headed north into the desert on foot. He looked back often.

By moonlight in the desert, far away from the prison, Joe saw a man, two horses and a pack mule, waiting for him. It was Bassett, a disheveled man in his fifties, looking more like a mountain man with his grey beard than a just-released convict.

Joe grinned as they connected. He looked back in the moonlight. No sign of trackers. Joe gladly mounted to rest his feet. They shook hands.

Bassett spoke with a drawl. "Your uncle sends his regards from Huntsville."

They rode in silence to avoid having their voices carry.

They rested at times but didn't camp. At daybreak, Bassett and Joe rode north across the red desert. They felt they were free and clear.

Joe gestured to him. "Anything's better than Huntsville, huh?"

"You got that right. They let me out after six months, but that was about all I could take. Heck, I mean, all I did was steal a horse."

"That so? Why didn't they hang you?"

"Just lucky I guess, but I told 'em I found it running loose." Bassett chuckled and looked back, then ahead. "I confused 'em. But you know, I got this thing about other folks' horses."

Joe reined up, looked back. So did Bassett. They were silent as they listened. No sign or sound of a hunt. They started riding again.

Bassett tugged at his hat brim. "Why wait for your uncle? You pay me enough, we could take Donovan now."

"They said to wait. I know better'n to cross 'im."

"Well, there's a little bank I know of that we could take, easy."

CHAPTER TWELVE

A few weeks later, in the desert with high winds and dust blowing, Joe Boot and Bassett rode wild through a rocky canyon. Joe had a money sack dangling from his saddle horn.

They came to a dead end. The walls were high, rugged.

Both men are out of breath and held onto their hats in the fierce wind. Their weary horses were drenched with sweat.

Joe looked up at the rocky terrain. "The horses can't make it up there."

"Yeah, well, that posse's hot on our heels. We got a choice?"

Bassett urged his horse up the wall of the canyon. Rocks and dirt flew beneath it's hooves as it struggled.

Joe panicked about being left behind and urged his horse up the wall. His mount fought the bit and tried to turn back. Dirt and rocks rolled under the hooves.

Bassett made it to the top of the wall. Then the mule made it.

Joe dug in his spurs, trying to keep going up the steep grade. His horse fell aside, jumped up, and shuddered. Blood poured out of its shoulder near where the money bag dangled.

Joe was still in the saddle, cussing under his breath.

The money bag, ripped open and off the saddle horn, fell into space and sailed downhill to the bottom of the canyon. As it landed, currency whipped about in the wind.

"There's the posse," Bassett said, gesturing back the way they had come. "Let's go!"

Frantic, Joe looked back down to see money flying everywhere.

Bassett, on the crest above, was cussing at him.

They could see the posse was coming fast from the desert. Joe grabbed at a few spiraling bills that spun up around them and managed to catch three.

Joe urged his wounded horse up the wall to join Bassett.

Bassett was furious. "I oughta knock your head off!"

Joe, sweating, rode onto the rise. "Yeah, let's get!"

Below, the posse was coming fast into the canyon. Money was still flying on the wind, right at the law.

Joe and Bassett crossed into a cluster of high red rocks and pines where they could not be seen and were able to escape to the west.

* * * *

Early spring of 1901 at Yuma, Guard Proctor brought Pearl an article from a newspaper and slid it through the bars to her.

"Thought you'd like to read what Joe Boot's been doing since he busted out. Him and another fellah are accused of robbing a bank."

Pearl stared at the article as Proctor continued.

"Seems the posse lost their trail but found the money floating down a steep rocky wall. Guess they lost it on the climb and were afraid to go back for it. When the local sheriff and posse tracked them to a bawdy house, they had already left, but one of the women knew it was Joe Boot and said he had bragged about having robbed a bank. Not real proof, but enough to make an arrest. Except Joe and his partner had plumb disappeared. Posse gave up."

"I thought maybe Joe was different."

"By the way, didn't you say he was waiting for an inheritance?"

"His grandfather. In Denver."

"They did some checking up there. Only time anyone ever heard of Joe Boot was in the Wild West Show passing through. Probably a stage name."

Pearl sadly took the news without too much surprise.

"What they did say was, he is greased lightning with a gun. Whatever he is now, he's on the run."

And that was all she knew of Joe's whereabouts.

*   *   *   *

On December 15, 1902, at Yuma prison, Pearl stood before the superintendent, who sat at the desk in his large office. It was nicely furnished and had wild west paintings on the wood-paneled walls, and white curtains framing a large window.

Wearing her nicest print dress, she waited, nervous, worried.

Next to Pearl stood Proctor, who looked very happy.

Pearl had no idea why she was there or what was tickling Procter. All she knew was, each time before this, she had lost another privilege. She had already been limited to one reporter a week, but that was fine with her.

Now she was afraid, because things had been going so well.

Superintendent Griffith—middle-aged, full beard with dark hair receding—held some important-looking documents in his hand. "Mrs. Hart, it seems half the state has been writing on your behalf. Your attorney also had great influence with a letter you had written Deputy Marshal Donovan, along with another letter from your brother. It seems your sentence was extremely harsh under the circumstances."

Pearl flushed with deep prayer in her heart.

Griffith held up the papers. "Governor Brodie has ordered parole for you."

Pearl was on the verge of collapse. Procter took her arm. She leaned on him as he helped her sit down, facing the desk. She was shaking, tearful, and still afraid.

Griffith continued. "There is one stipulation. You must leave Arizona Territory at once and not return until after the end of your five year sentence."

Pearl was trembling. Proctor stood close for comfort as Griffith sat back.

"Your lawyer found your sister is now living in Kansas City and contacted her. She is sending train tickets for you to join her and your mother there." Griffith paused, cleared his throat. "This will satisfy the conditions of your parole, which ends December, 1904. After that, you will be a free woman."

Pearl was falling apart. Proctor's hand was on her shoulder. She reached up to clasp it while tears trickled down her face.

Griffith handed over the documents, which Proctor reached for and then deposited in her hands. "You have any other plans?"

She wiped at her eyes. "I just want to be with my family."

"And your husband, have you heard from him?"

"No, and I hope I never do."

The superintendent handed her a paper to sign with pen and ink. She readily signed it, then sat back.

She wiped at her tears, smiled up at the grinning guard.

Abruptly, she got up, hugged the startled Proctor, who was armed.

Proctor quickly held her back at arms length and grinned.

"Thank you for your kindness," she said to him.

Pearl smiled, turned to look at the superintendent, who held up the palm of his hand to signify no hugging.

Pearl, papers in hand, walked to the door with Proctor. She paused as the superintendent came to walk her out. Pearl started out the door with the guard, stopped, whirled, grabbed the startled superintendent and hugged him with glee.

The superintendent looked over her head at Proctor and grinned, but he sobered as he pushed himself free. Pearl was so happy, she spun around and took Proctor's arm as they walked briskly down the hall.

One week later in Kansas City, at an old two-story house on a back street with lots of flowers, a wagon from the Union Pacific Railway station stopped in front as night fell. Pearl, wearing a duster over her dress and just off the train, sat next to the young, energetic driver. Her luggage was in the wagon bed. He hopped down, then gave her a hand to follow. He carried her luggage as she walked up to the front porch.

The driver set her luggage at her side, tipped his hat as she put coins in his hand, and went back to drive away.

Pearl, dressed nicely and wearing her hair in long curls under a little hat, took a deep, fearful breath, and knocked on the big oak door.

Within minutes, it opened. Her mother, sixty-eight-year-old Mrs. Taylor, a comely greying woman with a big smile and a sudden laugh, reached out to hug her.

Her sister, Mrs. Annie Frizzell, just turned forty-five, a pretty, classy lady in fine silk, hurried to join them and hug Pearl.

"We didn't expect you until tomorrow," her mother said with joy.

"I took an earlier train out of Tucson."

Annie was thrilled. "Mom, look at her. She's gorgeous."

They helped her bring in her luggage, then locked the door. They hugged her again with great affection. She took off her duster and they admired her blue dress.

"I made it myself," Pearl said. "The church in Globe sent me a lot of material."

"So lovely," her mother said.

They took her to the ornate parlor. Pearl sat on the soft green sofa with her mother. Annie brought tea and biscuits and set them on the coffee table in front of them, then sat on a stuffed chair near them.

"We thought you had cut yourself off from us," her sister said. "So many years of not answering our letters when we were in Canada. When we moved here, we decided to try writing the sheriff in Florence, and he sent our letter to your lawyer, who answered, and then he contacted the prison just before you were to be released. That's how we knew to send rail fare."

Pearl had tears in her eyes. "Annie, when you were living in Canada, I wrote almost every month until I finally gave up. Our brother is the only one who ever answered."

Annie caught her breath. "We never got your letters, ever, and we wrote to you, just the same."

"He was the only one to go to town for the mail," her mother said, tearful. "He always insisted. Now we know why."

Pearl was devastated. "I was so hurt, not hearing back from you. All he did was write to me for money. He said you were dying, Mom."

"I was sick for awhile, but that's all," her mother said.

Pearl leaned toward her mother, who hugged her.

"We're so glad to see you," Annie said. "This will be our first Christmas together in so many years!"

"And we're in a big city now," her mother added. "Electric lights. An automobile club. We're very modern."

Her sister brought more tea to the table, along with tea cake.

"Your children are still in school in Canada," their mother advised Pearl. "Your uncle Lawrence is their guardian now. He was the only one of us who had any funds to send them to school. But they will be here sometime this summer."

"Do they even want to see me?"

"They are a little older now, so I think they will understand in time," her mother replied. "But we are so sorry your brother lied to you."

"Where is he?" Pearl asked.

"Hiding in Canada," her mother said. "He has a drinking problem and he gambles. I cut him off to try to help him."

"I forgive him," Pearl said sadly. "It's the only way I can start over."

"I'm so sorry it ever happened," her mother said. "But you're here now and we're so glad."

"Will you miss the desert?" her sister asked, changing the subject.

"I will miss the red."

Her mother looked over at her sister. "Annie wants to tell you something."

Pearl waited with tea cup in hand as Annie looked about to bust with news.

"I wrote a play about your life," Annie said, leaning forward from her chair.

"What?"

"Wait until you read it. It will make you look like an innocent victim of Joe Boot and your brother's lies."

"Look like?" Pearl asked in dismay. "Annie, you need to hear the whole story."

"Yes, of course. I was only going by the newspapers and magazines."

Pearl leaned back where she sat on the sofa next to her mother.

Annie was still ecstatic. "We can fix it. We'll make it right. And they promised me we could put it on the first week in April. We can split the income from the show. It will help put you back on your feet."

"You really think people will come to see it?"

"Yes," Annie promised. "To see you. The heroine. And the villain, Joe Boot. And I gave you a great hero, a very wealthy man who rescues you."

Pearl shook her head. "But not for real. I always got the pretty ones who weren't good for anything. The bottom of the barrel. Never the big, solid hero."

The family was unaware of Chance Donovan, the man for whom Pearl yearned.

"What about Fred?" her mother queried. "Is he still in the Army?"

"Not for a long time, and I don't know where he is now,"

Pearl answered. "I hope I never see him again. He left me so many times, and then came back only for money. He'd beat me when I tried to stop him from taking my savings. Even left me unconscious one night at the hotel where I worked. That's why I sent my children to you, because I was afraid for them. And I heard that he's been in and out of jail for drinking and gambling."

Her sister was speechless with tears in her eyes.

Her mother was astonished. "We never knew."

Pearl murmured. "I was ashamed."

"Well, Kansas does not allow alcohol," her mother said. "Although men cross over to Missouri for it."

"If Fred comes here," her sister said, "we'll run him off."

Pearl was amused at her sister's belief that it was even possible. "All I can do is pray he never finds me."

* * * *

On the outskirts of Kansas City in 1903, Pearl's play premiered on April 5. It had attracted a lot of attention, particularly from newspapers and magazines

In front of the very large theater on a back street, the poster behind a glass frame read:

Coming soon: THE LADY BANDIT

It had a drawing of Pearl in boy's britches and a floppy hat, a bandana draped to the side of her face. She held a pistol in both hands.

*   *   *   *

In late March of that same year that Pearl's play would be shown, Chance Donovan was visiting the former Sheriff Truman in Florence. It was afternoon and clear.

Further down the street, and ducking into an alley, Joe Boot had been waiting for the sight of his intended victim. He circled around to the alley next to the entrance to Truman's office building and stayed in the shadows where he could listen.

No longer wearing a badge, Chance greeted his old friend on the boardwalk outside Truman's office, which had a new sign: Justice of the Peace. Truman was properly dressed as a peacemaker in his dark suit and no sidearm.

Waiting at the rail, Chance's buckskin was saddled with bedroll, possibles, and saddle bags, with a canteen dangling from the horn and a rifle in the scabbard. He now had the appearance of a rancher in his fringed buckskin jacket, red plaid shirt, and new wide-brimmed Stetson, but he still wore his sidearm.

Truman shook his hand. "I can't believe you hung up your badge."

Chance said, "You did. But why a Justice of the Peace now?"

"Judge asked me to pitch in, ease the calendar. Mostly, I just do weddings, or settle a dispute about a dog bite." Truman hesitated. "What are you going to do with yourself?"

"Going to settle down, buy a ranch, raise white face cattle." He turned to gesture at his buckskin. "Sam could use the rest in green pastures. Some peace and quiet. For both of us."

"Times are changing and getting more civilized every day, you know that. Electricity. More of them noisy motor cars smelling up the streets. Tourists with those little box cameras in your face. And we can't get rid of those ear-banging telephones."

Chance grinned. Green pastures sounded better by the minute.

Truman sobered. "One thing you should know—Joe Boot's hanging around again. Always asking folks if you're coming to town. He seems to have a bone to pick with you. Over Pearl?"

Chance shrugged, didn't answer or realize that Joe was listening in the nearby alley.

Pearl was out of reach for him and hopefully for Joe Boot. Chance had always had an urge to put his fist in the dandy's face.

Truman gave further warning. "He may be trouble if he's still in town."

"I'll be long gone."

"Not yet. I have a problem inside my office. Need your help."

Chance moved back to the center of the boardwalk and waited.

"Before we go inside, did you know? Pearl's in Kansas City, Kansas, with her family."

"Yes, I received the same report of her release from Yuma."

"Well, I had a deputy check up on her when he was there on assignment."

"And so?"

"He just got back. Seems she's doing a play about her life. The Lady Bandit. First week in April." He grinned, shook his head. "Maybe it'll be like one of those with the weeping heroine, the villain with the mustache, and the crowd booing. And the hero saves the day."

Chance had to grin. "She's full of surprises."

"Think the hero's going to look like a certain U.S. Marshal?"

That was too much for Chance. "Well, I just stopped to…"

"Hey, you can't leave just yet. Not until you talk to my visitors. Fred Hart's back in jail, and it took them years to track him down. Now they want him out and in their custody."

Chance winced at the name of Pearl's husband. It would ever be a painful thought to him.

"I need your help," Truman insisted.

Reluctant, Chance delayed his departure.

Inside the office in a simply furnished, back interview room, Chance joined Truman and stared at the visitors as he removed his hat.

Two well-dressed women were seated on the bench by the back window with red drapes closing off any view from the outside. Both blonde, pretty, and in their thirties, they wore feathered hats and a lot of lace.

Truman, for Chance's benefit, questioned them again. "Ladies, this here is retired U.S. Marshal Chance Donovan, Arizona Territory. For his benefit, lets get this straight. You are both still married to Fred Hart?"

Stunned, Chance could only react with dismay. His mouth went dry.

"Lucy Pride Hart," the younger one said. "1886. In Austin. We have a son."

"1887," said the other. "Janet Long Hart. Dallas."

"Pearl was married later on, in 1888," Truman said. "So, she was never legally wed."

Chance could barely control his emotions. He was certain his heart would beat itself to death. He had sweat on his brow. His hands ached.

"Fred Hart married each of them and stole their money,"

Truman said. "So, now I have their affidavits to that effect. He's still wed to Lucy here. So, he'll be charged with bigamy as to Janet and Pearl. But I'm sure the judge will agree to parole him into the custody of these nice ladies. They would surely make him pay."

Chance was speechless.

"Here are two extra copies of the affidavits," Truman said.

Chance accepted the documents, folded into an envelope, in a state of shock.

Truman grinned. "You take those to Pearl. I'll give you plenty of time to get there, and then I will send more copies to the local sheriff in Kansas City. Just for backup."

The two men came back outside into the sunlight. Chance was walking on air.

Both men were unaware Joe Boot was still listening in the next alley, hiding in the shadows.

"Take care of yourself, Chance. You're one of the last of the good guys." Truman gestured. "Are you taking the train to Kansas City?"

Chance shoved the affidavits inside his vest pocket. "No, I'll be riding all the way."

"You'll be making Pearl a very happy lady." Truman chuckled. "And her kids could use a proper name."

They walked to Chance's horse, still in earshot of Joe.

Chance finally grinned. "What do you think will happen to Fred Hart? You think he'll break parole to get away from those ladies?"

"Are you kidding? They're Texans. I'll bet they'll be armed. And they'll make him work off his debts. Not to mention, they both have fathers who are downright angry about the whole thing. They may want a piece of him, too."

Both men chuckled.

"So much for Fred Hart," Truman said with a wide grin.

Chance shook his hand. "No need telling anyone where I've gone."

"No, that would not be too smart. You're a free man now, on your own, headed for a new life. It's nobody's business but yours."

Chance mounted, paused, nodded at Truman, turned and rode northeast.

Truman folded his arms, watched Chance ride out of sight, then went back into his office.

Nearby in the shadows of the alley, Joe Boot, having had an earful, watched Chance leave.

Heading east and out to the prairie, Chance could barely contain his joy, knowing Pearl was free to marry. But why would she want a former lawman? She would be famous, starring in her own play. He would worry and fret every day and night on the trail.

Joe, however, had satisfied himself with where the Boxers could find Donovan.

Maybe now, once and for all, Joe's father would be avenged.

CHAPTER THIRTEEN

The next afternoon after Chance left for Kansas City, Truman returned to his office following his noon meal. He was happy because Fred Hart was now being escorted to Texas by his two wives and a deputy.

Waiting by Truman's desk was the young, freckled telegrapher, wearing a grey vest over his white shirt, and holding a telegram.

"Just came an hour ago. From Huntsville, Texas. The marshal can't be reached, so I gave it to the judge, and now he wants you to see it."

"Thanks." Truman opened it to see the time and date, 11:45 A.M., March 27, 1903. He read it aloud and was stunned. "Trey Boxer and his sons Rafe and Rufus escaped a work gang. Rip and Rory Boxer killed. Unknown help. Believe crossed into your territory."

"That's bad, I guess?" the young man asked.

"Could not be worse." Truman wiped his mouth with the back of his hand. "Well, sir, if anyone asks about where Chance Donovan is, you don't know."

The clerk look surprised. "How would I know where he is?"

"Let's hope no one does." Truman shook his head, knowing Chance had just left the day before and was still out in the middle of the prairie. "Get this back to your office and forward a copy to the U.S. Marshal in Phoenix."

"I tried. The line's not working. And the telephone is dead. They say it's because of high winds in the desert."

"Try again. Or send a messenger with it."

The telegrapher hurried back outside.

Truman sat down at his desk, knowing he had to take action to counter the Boxers if they came to his county. He stared at the telegram.

He picked up the hated shiny black telephone's receiver and put it to his ear. He heard nothing, and set it back on the cradle.

It would likely take Chance a week to get to Kansas City, just in time for the play.

No telling where the Boxers were now.

*   *   *   *

Northwest of Florence in rugged mountains on the following afternoon, Joe Boot was restless and pacing in a wooded clearing, where junipers and a few isolated cottonwoods stood among red streaked rocks and green grass. It was hot with no wind.

Spring water still ran down the nearby creek bed.

On his left stood an old shack, which had lost its window shutters and part of the roof, and the sheds near the single corral were in bad shape. A stone-circled well had allowed him to fill the nearby trough.

Once a handy hangout, it didn't have much comfort to offer.

He walked over to the shack where his horse was tied to the single rail. He checked his six-gun and adjusted his black hat. His wore his usual dandy's outfit with shiny red vest. Impatient, he stared down the slope along the empty trail.

He started to go back inside, stopped, and looked again.

Dust rose on the near-barren desert, far beyond. Three riders were coming his way.

Hairy, fierce men on weary horses, the Boxers were worn and ragged. Trey was in the lead, followed by his sons, Rufus and Rafe. They were dirty and grimy in ill-fitting clothes, but they were well-armed.

They saw Joe waving from the rise and reined up together, resting their mounts as they waved back.

Rafe chuckled. "There's our little cousin. He sure looks like he's been living the good life."

Rufus agreed. "The kid's got talent. But he ain't never killed nobody. I don't figure he's had the guts to kill Donovan."

"He's got enough reason."

"I got first call," Trey said. "Randy was my kid brother."

His sons fell silent. They knew Trey had lost four brothers, all told, to various shootouts over the years. Randy had been the youngest of the five and was Trey's favorite. Not to mention Trey had also just lost two sons when escaping the Texas work gang.

"Don't worry, Pa. If Joe didn't get Donovan, we will," Rafe said.

They rode up to where Joe stood beaming at their arrival and dismounted.

"I was getting worried," Joe said as Trey came over to shake his hand. "Those were two good men I paid off to get you free."

"They were shot down," Trey said. "So were Rory and Rip. We're all that's left. But we figure we're in the clear by now."

Joe winced. "Gees, Uncle Trey, I'm right sorry. But where's Bassett?"

"Never showed. Off somewhere stealing horses, I reckon. We won't see him again."

"What about Donovan? Is he dead?"

Joe shrugged and shook his head.

Rafe scratched his chest and eyed the trough. "You got fresh clothes for us?"

"In the cabin. And hot coffee and grub."

"Take care of these horses first," Trey said to his sons.

An hour later, inside the grimy one-room cabin, where the iron stove had allowed a hot meal and coffee, the Boxers relaxed on broken furniture.

Trey had a one-track mind. "Now we got to find Donovan."

Joe, seated on a stool, grinned. "I have some good news. Pearl Hart's in Kansas City, Kansas."

"Why is that good news?" Trey grunted. "She's just another female."

"Yeah," Rafe said, "why do we even care?"

Joe looked puffed up. "On account of Donovan's on his way there. He left two days ago. I overheard him say he was riding alone, all the way."

"How we gonna find him?" Trey asked.

"We don't," Joe said. "We take the train and get to Kansas City about the same time. Wherever Pearl is, that's where he'll be."

"What's she got to do with it?" Rufus wanted to know.

"Donovan's smitten with her."

"Big city," Trey said. "She could be anywhere."

"She's putting on a stage play about her life," Joe said. "Easy to find."

"Why don't they do a show about us?" Rafe grumbled.

"Kansas City," Trey mused. "No one knows us there."

"And after we get Donovan, we can go on up north," Joe said.

Trey readily agreed. "I hear they got so many cattle in Wyoming and Montana, they lost count."

"They also got vigilantes," Rafe reminded his father.

"We'll worry about that when we get there," Trey said. "First, we find Donovan. He's gonna pay for killing my kid brother. And hauling us off to Yuma."

"I get first crack," Joe said. "It's my pa he killed."

"You're a trick shot artist on the stage," Trey said. "You get up there and shoot dancing balls and some targets. You draw real fast, but you ain't never shot a man."

"Until now," Joe insisted.

Rafe downed his coffee. "Oh, let him try, Pa."

"Yeah," Rufus added. "We'll be right behind him."

Joe appeared to feel important, but inside, he knew they were right. He had never shot a man because he had managed to avoid it until now.

If he admitted the truth, he was scared silly of Donovan.

*   *   *   *

Unaware the Boxers had busted out and were on his trail, Chance enjoyed crossing hundreds of miles across the country he loved. He avoided all civilization except for supplies. He found nights on the prairie to be peaceful, except for coyotes and other critters.

Sunrises and sunsets were colorful and calm.

In Missouri, he helped a farmer corral some runaway sheep and was invited for a hot meal, bath, and a cot in the barn. In Wichita, he stocked up for the rest of his trip.

Happy he was the one to bring her good news, he kept up a steady pace. He had no idea when her play would be staged. Nights, he sat by his campfire, poked at the burning chips with a stick, and studied the stars in the dark sky. He talked to Sam, who seemed to understand.

He often took out his father's gold watch and gazed at it. He thought back to being that skinny little orphan found near death in the wasteland. The big ranger who saved and adopted him but was later murdered.

Even further back, the night his mother had been knocked down the stairs by his drunken stepfather. The night she had died. He still had years of whip marks on his back. The scar of a bullet hole when he had been shot in the back while escaping.

He thought of Pearl. He carried the affidavits for her, proof she had never been married to Fred Hart. She was free to live a new life.

Chance hoped he would make an offer she would accept.

* * * *

There was wind and rain that morning on April 5, 1903, in Kansas City, but it had subsided by noon. The Star Theater stood on the north side of a back street where other buildings stood empty, weather-beaten, and abandoned.

Wagons and gas buggies lined the street across from the theater, next to an empty two-story hotel where saddle horses lined a long rail. Chance's buckskin stood at the far end. 'No parking' signs were on the theater side of the street so that the curb was free of vehicles.

A large crowd had gathered and entered for the two o'clock matinee of a new production, a play called The Lady Bandit.

Clouds were moving back in as the wind rose.

Inside the large theater, there were high windows opened for cooling air.

The curtains closed across the wide stage were a deep maroon.

Refreshments were at a counter in the back, to the right when standing at the entrance and looking at the stage. It was where the overflow crowd had to stand.

Chance Donovan, no longer wearing a badge, hovered in the shadows in a far corner to the left of the entrance.

The director, an important-looking man with a goatee, wearing a grey suit, came out in front of the curtain and spoke.

"Ladies and gentlemen, welcome to the true story of Pearl Hart, a lady with an abusive husband, in desperate need of money, who was told that her mother was dying in Canada. When the mines closed down, she lost her job as a cook and had nowhere to turn except for a gambler named Joe Boot, who had befriended her. Now you will see what followed in her life."

On stage, a simulated cardboard stagecoach without horses, managed from behind by unseen hands, rolled into view. Phony trees and brush covered the back wall.

The driver, sitting on a makeshift wagon seat, held up by an hidden stepladder on a rolling platform, wore a big, handlebar mustache, and a long, black coat. He held lines as if there were horses. The coach had a door and window through which men could be seen inside.

Out of the brush, the actor playing Joe Boot sprang forth on foot, six-gun in hand. He wore a fiery red vest and a silver-studded gunbelt. He also wore a big sombrero and thick, black handlebar mustache, obviously a prop. He carried a gunny sack in his left hand.

"Hold up!" Joe Boot the actor called.

The driver simulated pulling the horses to a halt.

Joe the actor moved around to the front of the stage, standing sideways to the audience. He held his pistol on the driver, who held up his hands.

The real Pearl Hart, in boys' clothes, hair up under a wide brimmed man's hat, came out behind the brush in the rear and remained in the background. She held a pistol in both hands. Their faces were covered by red bandanas.

The driver threw up his hands. He remained in front of the coach image as if on the seat. Through a cardboard door behind him, the passengers peered out the open window.

The actor Joe Boot barked at the passengers, "Everybody out!"

Three white male passengers and a Chinaman stepped out through the cardboard door, hands in the air. The Chinaman stood bowlegged and silent.

One, a chubby white man with a bowler hat and bow tie, quivered in his boots and pleaded, "Please don't shoot."

Another, a skinny man in an outrageous plaid suit, looked around furtively. "All I have is a dollar."

The third white man just looked scared.

Joe the actor robbed the men of their money, pistols, and valuables, shoving it all in the gunny sack. Pearl continued to hold her pistol on them and remained far back.

Standing in the rear of the theater in the dark corner, Chance, hat in hand, cringed at the scene, then suddenly found himself grinning.

On stage, Joe demanded of the driver, "Throw down your pistol."

The driver obeyed, and Joe kicked it over to Pearl, who picked it up.

Joe continued with the driver. "Throw down the strong box."

"Don't have one. Just the mail sack."

"Throw it down!"

The driver reached toward the front of the stage, where he was secretly handed the mail bag. He threw it so it fell near Joe's boots.

Joe the actor grabbed the mail bag and pulled out a handful of letters. He tore some of them open and found some paper money, which he shoved in the gunny sack.

The driver shouted, "Give it back, or the federal law will be on you."

Joe the actor shoved unopened mail back into the mail bag and tossed it back to the driver. "Now get! All of you!"

The passengers fell all over themselves, getting back into the coach.

The driver picked up the lines and "drove" off the stage to the right.

Joe the actor and Pearl stood watching it leave. Alone on the stage, they dropped their bandanas.

"We done it, Pearl," he said as he scooped the money from

the bag of valuables and shoved it into his pockets. "We got over four hundred dollars."

"What are you doing? I want my share. You know my mother's going to die if I don't send it on. You promised."

"I lied to you, Pearl. There's a big poker game."

"No, Joe, please!"

The crowd booed Joe Boot the actor.

Out of the brush stepped a big lawman with handlebar mustache and a huge badge. A posse of three heavily-bearded men, also with badges, stood behind him.

They all had big guns aimed at Pearl and Joe the actor.

Pearl and Joe dropped their weapons, raised their hands.

The curtain went down. The crowd applauded.

Still unnoticed, Chance leaned against the back wall, grinning, and shook his head.

After a short while, the curtain rose to a simulated courtroom.

Pearl stood in front of the judge's high desk where he sat on a stool. The judge had a mean face and beard. "I gave your partner thirty years. What have you to say?"

She pleaded her case.

"Your Honor, women did not vote for your laws. I should not be bound by them."

Her attorney, important looking, complained. "She was a victim, your honor."

"Five years."

After more argument, the curtain closed.

The director then appeared in front of the curtain. "Please enjoy the intermission. Pearl will be back with the rest of her true story."

Intermission allowed everyone to stand and stretch. Some enjoyed the refreshments in the back of the theater. Through the high windows, they saw dark clouds moving in. No one ventured out in the wind, which rose to rattle the heavily-shaded front windows.

Chance avoided the crowd and stood in the shadows.

In rising wind under a now cloudy sky, four riders rode into the street from the west. The theater was on their left. They saw the poster for THE LADY BANDIT under glass by the front door.

They reined up near the alley on the theater's right side.

Trey Boxer, his sons Rafe and Rufus, along with Joe Boot, looked around the street at the abandoned hotel and the front rail lined with saddle horses.

Joe pointed. "The buckskin, that's Donovan's."

Trey directed his sons to cross over with their horses, tether them at the next building's rail, and get on the veranda of the empty hotel. They could see broken windows, cracked front steps, and a crooked post barely holding the porch roof. On the left side of the hotel, there were steps leading to the second floor.

He and Joe took the alley next to the theater and to its right. Trey stopped at the alley entrance behind some empty crates.

"Might be a long wait," Trey said.

"He's gotta come out some time."

Joe noticed that even further back in the alley, two boys, around ten years of age and wearing shabby clothes, had pushed barrels together with a board across them. They were standing on a wooden box on top of the board and were peeking in the high window at the show. The roof overhang protected them from the threat of rain but the wind tore at them.

In time, the sunlight reappeared as the clouds moved on, and the wind slowly wound down to a breeze.

Hearing applause inside the theater, Joe grumbled that he was missing the show.

Joe kicked a rock. It hit the wall near the boys, who got skittish, scrambled down, and ran out the back of the alley. Joe removed the box, got up on the board, and peered into the theater.

As the second act began, Joe saw himself step on stage, dressed like a dandy. The crowd booed.

One of the barrels suddenly gave way, and the board dipped. He danced back over to the other barrel and slid sideways as it also collapsed.

He wobbled. "Yikes!"

He fell haphazardly and landed on his rear.

Trey turned to glare at him, waved him to be silent. Trey went back to watching the street, but this time he was grinning. Joe never failed to entertain.

Joe recovered his dignity and came up behind his uncle. They could see Rufus and Rafe huddled down on the veranda across the street.

"Gonna be too many witnesses," Trey said.

Joe tensed, waiting for his uncle to continue.

"You're ten times faster than any man alive, including Donovan. Just make it a fair fight so no one can make a fuss." Trey hesitated. "If you can pull the trigger."

"He shot my father," Joe said with bravado. "He'll be dead before he can slap leather."

"What about the woman?"

"I got some unfinished business with her."

CHAPTER FOURTEEN

While the show continued inside the theater in Kansas City, Rafe and Rufus Boxer were positioned across the street, hiding on the veranda of the abandoned hotel across from the theater. Saddle horses lined the rail in front and below.

Buggies and motor cars were parked further up the street from the hotel in the afternoon sun. The street was still muddy from the recent rain. Sunlight had returned as the clouds moved on, and the wind was only a breeze once more.

In the alley next to the theater to the right of the entrance, Trey and Joe waited for signs of Chance Donovan.

Inside the theater, Chance remained out of sight in the dark corner to the right of the entrance. Hat in hand, he wore a long black coat over his blue plaid shirt. He was wearing his side arm but no badge.

On stage as the show continued, a large painting of the front gate of Yuma Prison dressed the rear wall. Pearl stood with her luggage and purse in front of the backdrop.

Joe Boot the actor, now wearing twin holsters, entered from the left and hurried up to her on foot. "I escaped a long time ago, Pearl, but I came back for you."

"You're only here for the money."

Joe the actor feigned surprise. "What money?"

"The money all the people sent me. The money I'm sending to my mother. And for my children."

"We need all of it, Pearl. It will take us to California."

"Go away!"

Actor Joe grabbed at her purse, tried to take it away from her.

The audience booed. Pearl fought to hold onto her purse.

From behind them came a big, handsome actor dressed like a wealthy man with gold watch and chain. He carried a cane trimmed in gold. "Unhand that woman!"

Joe Boot the actor backed off and drew his six-gun.

The hero with the cane used it to knock the gun from Joe's hand. It went sailing away.

The audience cheered.

Joe Boot the actor pulled his other six-gun, fired with a loud pop.

The hero staggered a bit, recoiled, slammed down the gun with his cane, then beat on Joe Boot the actor until he was on his knees. "Be gone!"

Joe Boot the actor crawled away without his guns.

The hero kicked Joe Boot the actor in the rear as he then scrambled out of sight.

The audience cheered. The hero took Pearl in his arms.

The curtain closed, then reopened, as Pearl and the male actors took a bow to loud applause. Then the curtain closed.

The director reappeared in front of the curtains. "Please stay in your seats. Pearl Hart will return in a few minutes with the continuing story of her adventure."

When the curtain reopened, Pearl was standing alone in a pretty blue dress with lace and wearing a bonnet.

She continued her story as the crowd fell silent.

"Yuma prison was hot every day, freezing every night. It was dusty all the time. We had bedbugs and termites. Every manner of critter."

She paused, the memories still painful.

"The food was either fair or terrible. For breakfast, we had beef hash and wheat bread. For supper, if we were lucky, we'd have roast beef and mashed potatoes. Or something that looked an awful lot like scorpions and rats."

The crowd was silent, as was Chance in the dark corner.

"But we had electricity, and a blower would send some air into the cells. I was allowed to wear my own clothes. I sang in the choir. It was spiritual, singing to those forsaken men. They let me leave because so many wonderful people had taken my side with the governor. And now I'm home. In Kansas City, the real Pearl of the West."

She took many bows to the applause before the curtain closed in front of her.

The crowd filed out to head for home.

Lights were turned up bright. A cast party was taking place on the stage behind partially opened curtains.

Chance, alone at the rear of the empty theater, could see actors dancing around with glasses of something in hand. Joe the Actor was swinging about in triumph.

He saw Pearl, wearing a green dress and looking happy, forward of the cast and crew. She had her back to him and was talking to two ladies in street dress, but he was unaware they were her mother and sister. As the party continued, a seemingly overwhelmed Pearl turned to the front of the stage to look at the empty seats.

Now she saw Chance, who had stepped forward into the light, just short of the aisles that led toward the stage. He was standing, hat in hand.

With great joy, she turned to the two ladies, spoke to them, and ran off the stage and down the steps. Her mother and sister stared after her.

Pearl could hardly breathe as she hurried down the aisle. Within ten feet of him, she slowed and stopped. "Marshal!"

He came forward, closer, with a big smile on his face.

Pearl had never seen him so relaxed and cheerful.

"What did you think of my play?" she asked.

"It was kind of... fun."

She laughed. "It was supposed to be serious."

"I know."

"Come, I want you to meet my mother and sister."

"Not now. I have news. Better said outside."

"Is it cold?"

He took off his long coat and, moving behind her, put it over her shoulders.

"This won't take long."

She smiled at the thought and walked out into the hazy sunlight with him. They stood in the recess with their backs to the theater doors.

They were not aware of the Boxer brothers on the veranda of the abandoned hotel across the street, nor that Trey and Joe were in the alley to their left.

The street had emptied of buggies and motor cars. Only Chance's buckskin was at the rail by the hotel. The outlaws had hidden their mounts.

Chance and Pearl now moved forward into the sunlight and on the boardwalk.

Pearl, wearing his long coat, was so excited to see Chance, she could barely keep from squealing her joy and reaching for him. Hat in hand, he adored the sight of her.

His heart was pounding so loud it echoed in his ears. He felt cold all over.

"I'm so glad to see you," she said. "I just received a letter changing my status and advancing a full pardon, so I'm free!"

"I have other news."

"You're not a marshal anymore?"

"No, I bought a ranch."

"That's wonderful." She was afraid to ask to go with him.

He fought to say more and finally spoke. "It's about Fred Hart."

She winced as he drew out an envelope. He reached in to pull out the affidavits.

'No,' she thought. 'Don't let him find me. Please.'

She fearfully accepted and read the two papers without understanding their full meaning because they put her in shock. She folded them and gazed at Chance, waiting for him to explain, which he did with a happy heart.

He reached out for them and put them back in the envelope for her. He slid them back in his vest. Now he forced himself to get out the story.

"Fred Hart already had two other wives before he married you."

She gasped. "What does that mean?"

"You're not married."

"I'm free?"

"Yes."

Pearl hugged herself but ached to hug him instead. "What will happen to him?"

"His two wives found him in jail. I think the first was a shotgun wedding. He's being charged with bigamy but was released to their custody. I think he's going to have to pay for what he did, whichever way they and their families decide. I think there are a couple of fathers in Texas with plans for him. Maybe he'll be picking cotton."

"I'm so blessed." Then her smile faded into misery. "But now my children, they were born out of wedlock. They'll be shamed."

"You could get married. And your husband could adopt them. Give them a new name. A new life."

"Who would want me now?"

Chance had trouble pulling himself together. He had ridden all the way from Florence to deliver a message and ask her to marry him. But now he was like a quaking aspen.

"Mr. Donovan, are you all right?"

"Yeah, I..."

"Are you sure? I mean, your face is so red."

Chance looked around, saw no one. He began to fumble his words.

"I know it's kind of sudden, but on the other hand, it's not. I mean, I've been thinking about it since I first saw you crawling in the mud." Now he lost his courage. "I mean, I thought... if you would..."

Pearl moved closer, peered up at him. He pushed his hat back on his head.

Pearl Hart & the Violent Men

"Chance Donovan, are you asking me to marry you?"

"Yeah," he mumbled. "I mean, I got the ranch, if you—"

"Yes!"

He was so startled, he barely realized she had rushed into his arms and was on her tiptoes. He held her as gently as he could, but he was badly shaken. She felt like the world in his arms.

Now she reached up and he bent down so their lips could meet.

It had taken nearly five years to get from finding her in the mud to this moment. He could not believe it was happening. His heart was racing. His chest hurt. He felt a chill run through him.

Pearl was overwhelmed with his passionate kiss. She had lived a terrible life, just for this wonderful moment. Both were breathing silent prayers of thanks.

Pearl's heart was singing. She was shivering, trembling, ecstatic.

She felt warm and tender and alive in his embrace.

Kissing and hugging her in a daze, Chance was unaware of the coming danger.

"You really want to adopt my children?" she asked, her face at his chest.

He caressed her soft hair. "Yes, they'll do well on the ranch."

"Freddy hates being called Fred."

"When I was a kid, my name was Wesley."

"Wes! He would love that."

So full of joy, they kissed again.

"Donovan!" came a sharp voice behind Pearl, from the direction of the alley.

Chance stiffened. He was wearing his side arm, but that

wasn't his hesitation. He was finally holding the first and only love of his life.

Carefully, Chance pushed her back toward the entrance. "Get inside."

Pearl moved back into the recessed entrance and stopped near the door but didn't do as he said.

Joe Boot, drumming up all his courage, stood some fifteen feet away, not wearing his coat. Hands down by his twin holsters, his face shaded by his hat, he fought the urge to back away. He knew Trey was watching and listening. He was more afraid of his uncle than the lawman. Sweat formed on his brow.

"I've been looking for you, Donovan."

Behind Joe at the alley entrance, Trey Boxer stayed out of sight. Trey's sons watched from the veranda across the street. The sun was bright with rising wind. Not even Joe carried as much hate for Randy's killer as Trey.

Joe moved forward a few more steps onto the boardwalk. He was showing off now, for his uncle and cousins, and for Pearl. His carefree demeanor was gone. He was beginning to like his part. He postured.

"Joe!" Pearl called, frightened. "He's not a lawman anymore."

"He killed my father," Joe said. "Randy Boxer, down in Texas."

Chance wasn't that surprised. "He was robbing a bank. They killed five people, including a woman who was with child."

Joe didn't care who else died at the bank, but didn't mind a delay to allow him to fight for more courage. He snarled at Chance.

"He was my pa, and you're gonna pay for it."

"You had my father's gold watch," Chance countered. "Where'd you get it?"

Joe snickered. "That ranger was your pa? We shot him down, yeah, but he was the wrong Donovan, so that don't make us even, because he was a stinking ranger, and my Pa was a better man."

Pearl put her hand over her mouth to stifle a cry. She knew Chance was aware Joe was a trick shot artist, a showman, a fast draw.

Joe was aware his cousins were watching from the far veranda. He knew Trey was behind him in the alley. He had to show them he was just as much a man as any of them.

Yet, he was losing his drummed-up courage, so he had to get it done.

"Draw first or I will!" Joe said.

Suddenly braver at Chance's hesitation, Joe whipped out his right six-gun with lightning speed. But before he could fire, Chance had already drawn and pulled the trigger.

Joe gasped in disbelief. He was hit in his chest, dead center. He fired into the boardwalk. He stared at Chance with wide-eyed amazement. How could anyone be faster than Joe Boot?

Joe was dying on his feet. He waved his six-gun, lost control of it. His weapon flew sideways, over near where Pearl cowered.

As Joe fell in a heap and lay dead on the boardwalk, his cousins fired from the veranda across the street. One shot grazed Chance, who was unaware that another shot had hit Pearl. She sank to one knee with blood on her bodice.

It was hard to see the brothers because of the ornate woodwork on the rim of the veranda. Chance waited until he saw movement, two dark shapes, low on the platform.

Chance fired, hit Rafe in the forehead, knocked him back.

Rufus, hunched down, fired and missed. Chance fired back,

hit him in the face. Rufus jerked and dropped, dying along side his brother.

Chance glanced at the nearby rooftops, at the alleys, the windows, and down the street.

Trey, hidden in the alley, was so distraught, it took a long moment for him to recover. He had now lost all four of his sons and his brother, and his brother's son, too. Donovan had to die. He wiped his hands on his shirt to be sure they were dry.

Chance was suddenly aware that the cast and crew had appeared at the far side of the theater. They had exited the stage door and worked their way around. Now they backed away but three of the actors stayed at the edge as witnesses. Others, along with Pearl's mother and sister, hovered behind them. They could not see Pearl.

In front of the theater entrance, even though wounded, Pearl, on one knee, reached over to recover Joe's pistol and drew back the hammer. She rose up against the theater wall, resting against it.

Chance holstered his revolver and was about to turn to check on Pearl when Trey Boxer, six-gun in hand, came out of the same alley from which Joe had appeared.

"Don't move!" Trey said. Looking like death itself, Trey stopped on the boardwalk and aimed at Chance.

Chance had his right hand near his holster and weighed his chances.

"So that other Donovan was your pa," Trey sneered. "Yeah, we took his watch. And now you're gonna meet up with him, wherever he is. You're dead, marshal."

After a lifetime of being haunted by the memory of this man, Chance now had it driving him to get it said.

"He found me in the desert. With a bullet in my back. Your bullet."

Trey made a face. "What?"

"I still have scars on my back from your bullwhip."

Still not getting it, Trey kept his aim on Chance but looked odd. This really tall and husky lawman bore no resemblance to the skinny little kid Trey had whipped.

"You were drunk that night. My mother died when you pushed her down the stairs," Chance said with venom. "I was twelve years old."

"What the devil?"

Chance waited until his enemy began to remember, then hit him with it.

"You were my stepfather."

Trey was speechless but still deadly.

Both men were unaware of the wounded Pearl holding Joe's pistol where she stood, leaning back on the theater wall. She slid down to sit against it. She was bleeding and getting weaker by the moment.

Trey Boxer was still having trouble accepting this big man as the skinny Wes.

"You were her kid?" Trey asked, shaking his head.

"Wesley."

"All these years?"

Chance knew that Trey was about to pull the trigger. He weighed his chances of drawing in time or dodging until he could.

Trey's eyes said he was going to fire. And he would have, but he was shot in his right thigh from Joe's pistol, weaving in Pearl's hands. She then collapsed.

Trey gasped in pain from his wobbly leg but only glanced at her. He knew he'd better kill Chance right now.

Chance drew and jumped aside as Trey fired and missed. Chance shot Trey in the chest, dead center.

Trey stared at him, fell back, fired at the sky, and died on his feet as he crashed down. He slowly rolled off the boardwalk into the muddy street.

Joe Boot and the Boxers were gone forever.

The cast and crew appeared from behind the far edge of the theater. Pearl's mother and sister were right on their heels.

Chance, realizing Pearl had saved his life, turned to go to her, only to see her lying on her side, still holding Joe's weapon, near the theater wall.

She gazed at him with love, and then her eyes closed.

He rushed to kneel at her side, lifting her in his arms in a terrible panic.

"Pearl! Don't die on me!"

*   *   *   *

Back to 1910 at the Bear Springs Ranch with Chance and the reporter having lemonade in the late afternoon sun, under the watchful eyes of a big white dog...

Elmer was so wound up, he could hardly get his words out.

"My gosh, what happened to Pearl? Did she die?"

"No."

"Thank God, and I can't believe Trey Boxer was your stepfather!"

"Neither could he."

"That's so huge. Can I write it?"

"As long as I see it first."

"So where is Pearl?" Elmer persisted.

"She remarried."

"But what happened to Fred Hart?"

"I heard he's still picking cotton for his first wife's father, down in Texas."

"That's a real comedown." Elmer enjoyed the thought.

At that moment, the teenage girl and her younger brother rode by at a fast trot, waving, and then into a gallop, heading for greener pastures.

"Yours?" Elmer asked.

"Adopted. Nellie was named after her grandmother, so she kept it. Young Fred changed his name to Wesley."

"Wait, you adopted Pearl's kids?"

"We're all Donovans now."

Elmer got unbearably excited. "So where is Pearl?"

At that moment, they heard small boys squabbling inside and a woman telling them to behave. Elmer was awestruck.

"Twin boys," Chance said with a grin. "They're four now."

At that moment, Pearl, wearing a printed apron over her blue dress, came outside with a ten-month-old girl with dark curly hair, now resting on her right hip. Her own long, dark hair was tied back with a ribbon. She had cake flour on her left cheek. She looked beautiful.

Elmer stood, hat in hand, his mouth open.

Running around her were two freckle-faced boys with auburn hair and big blue eyes. Wearing denim pants and checkered shirts, they were laughing and arguing. They ran over to Chance and pushed at each other as they both scrambled onto his knees. Then they burst out laughing as he grinned. They jumped off and ran down the steps and into the garden, one chasing the other.

The big, white dog just watched.

"My wife, Pearl," Chance said, still with a grin. "Elmer Kitchen."

Elmer nearly choked. "Wow."

"Annie won't nap inside," Pearl said, depositing the little girl on Chance's lap, where the child folded against him and promptly went to sleep in his arms.

Pearl then returned inside. They could smell something wonderful, which was beef roast in the oven.

"My gosh," Elmer said, sinking back down on his chair. He was so excited he could hardly contain himself. "Pearl? She is so beautiful."

"And still sings," Chance said, holding his daughter safely as she slept, "but only here with us. On Sundays."

"That's amazing."

They paused to watch the young twin boys playing in the garden.

"You must be a happy man," Elmer said.

"It was all worth it."

Elmer poured them both more lemonade.

Shortly thereafter, Pearl came outside. Elmer stood up again, hat in hand.

She walked around to stand between the dog and Chance's chair. She leaned down to kiss his forehead.

"Elmer is a reporter," Chance told her. "He's writing our story, but we have approval rights."

"Did you tell him you chased me for years?" she asked, laughing.

They kissed as if Elmer wasn't there.

"You have a big family now," Elmer offered.

"Yes," she said. "Chance adopted my children, and now we have three of our own, so far."

Elmer looked surprised. "So far?"

Pearl smiled. "I hope it's another girl."

Chance, wide-eyed, half rose. "What?"

Elmer grinned from ear to ear as he watched them kiss again.

"Seven months from now," she said to Chance. "I wanted to be sure before I told you."

Chance was speechless. He was a supremely happy man.

She turned to Elmer. "You must stay for supper. And the night. We have lots of room."

"My pleasure," Elmer said, grateful for his good fortune.

"And now, Mr. Kitchen," she said, "I need someone to peel the potatoes."

She kissed Chance again and went inside. Elmer readily left his paperwork to follow.

Chance was alone with his little girl sound asleep in his lap, and with his big white dog, also asleep. He could see their twin boys still playing in the garden, and also the teens, who had circled the house and ridden back to the corrals.

He smiled as he watched his buckskin grazing on the golden hillside where white face cattle wandered about. Dark clouds had reached the crimson bluffs on the far northern horizon.

Leaning back, he felt like the happiest man in the world. Both he and Pearl would always remember the past, but those painful memories were far behind them.

He chose instead to only remember the first day he had seen Pearl, crawling in the mud. Sitting down in the bathtub with water splashing over the sides. So defiant and pretty. Hearing her sing. And seeing her on the stage in Kansas City. Then outside the theater, saying yes to him. He chose not to think of the shooting.

Instead, he smiled as he remembered Truman standing proud as his best man. Her sister Annie had been her maid of honor, with Pearl so beautiful in an ivory, lace-trimmed gown at their church wedding. Her mother had cried the whole time.

From then on, their life had been every lonely man's dream.

His daughter stirred in his arms but continued to sleep.

Chance closed his eyes. He whispered his thanks in prayer.

He was a happy and very grateful man.

ABOUT THE AUTHOR

Western novelist and screenwriter **Lee Martin** grew up on cattle ranches in Northern California. *Pearl Hart & the Violent Men* will be Martin's 29th traditional Western novel, which is also written as a screenplay. Martin concentrates on action Western scripts, but also writes in other genres.

Martin's credits include three Western movies now produced.

The Desperate Riders, written by Lee Martin and based on Martin's novel, produced and directed by Michael Feifer in Tennessee, was released February 25, 2022. Stars include Drew Waters, Trace Adkins, Tom Berenger, Vanessa Evigan, Sam Ashby, Victoria Pratt, Cowboy Troy, Rob Mayes, Brock O'Hurn and Peter Sherayko.

Martin's novel *The Siege at Rhyker's Station*, with a screenplay by Lee Martin, was filmed in the mountains of Southern California. It was released in December of 2021 as *Last Shoot Out*, produced and directed by Michael Feifer, and stars Brock Harris, Skylar Witte, Peter Sherayko, Jay Pickett, David Deluise, Michael Welch, Brock Burnett, Caia Coley, Keikilani Grune, Jerry Bestpitch, Cam Gigandet, and the legendary Bruce Dern. It received a great review in *Variety*. And Martin has just been awarded a Spur Award by Western Writers of America for the Best Western Screenplay.

Martin's screenplay for **Shadow on the Mesa**, starring Kevin Sorbo, Wes Brown, and Gail O'Grady, was based on Martin's novel of the same title (first edition published by Five Star Publishing, 2014). The movie was the second-highest-rated and second-most-watched original movie in Hallmark Movie Channel's history when it premiered in 2013. The film also won the prestigious Wrangler Award given by the National Cowboy & Western Heritage Museum in Oklahoma City for Best Original TV Western Movie. The novel is now available in paperback and ebook.

Hang Town, one of Martin's most recent novels, now also optioned for the screen, received a fine review from Western Writers of America: "Lee Martin gives the reader a plot and a cast of characters ready-made for a riveting teleplay. Action, romance, and revelation appear on every page." —Robert Dwyer, *Roundup Magazine*.

In Mysterious Ways, Martin's new modern suspense Western, received great critical acclaim from both *Kirkus Reviews* and *Midwest Book Reviews*.

A review from Western Writers of America said of *In Mysterious Ways*: "Lee Martin, best known for fast-paced traditional Westerns, turns to contemporary California in this thriller. The plot involves a young woman, abandoned at birth, and her young son; an Army Veteran-turned-rancher who says the girl is the spitting image of his long-lost love; and a scheming ne'er-do-well who believes the girl is from a rich family and will stop at nothing to get rich quick. Throw in a kind-hearted deputy, the villain's sister, a local festival at a small lake town and you get an-easy-to-read novel that will appeal to fans who like thrillers that are character-driven, without profanity or graphic violence and end with the quintessential happy-ever-after (unless you're rooting for the bad guy) —Johnny D. Boggs, Editor, *Roundup Magazine*, August 2022.

Martin is always working on the next novel and screenplay. For the latest news, follow Lee Martin Westerns on Facebook.